Lesser Light

by Matthew Drapper

Copyright

First Printing: 2022
ISBN: 978-1-3999-3957-7
Buxton, United Kingdom. Benson Frisbee.
www.bensonfrisbee.com
info@bensonfrisbee.com
Copyright © 2022 by Matthew Drapper
Publisher: Benson Frisbee
Cover art © Matthew Drapper

Dedicated to all who lost their lives to gain nothing.

CHAPTER 1...11

CHAPTER 2...19

CHAPTER 3...25

CHAPTER 4...37

CHAPTER 5...41

CHAPTER 6...45

CHAPTER 7...51

CHAPTER 8...59

CHAPTER 9...63

CHAPTER 10...71

CHAPTER 11...77

CHAPTER 12...81

CHAPTER 13...89

CHAPTER 14 95

CHAPTER 15 99

CHAPTER 16 103

CHAPTER 17 107

CHAPTER 18 111

CHAPTER 19 115

CHAPTER 20 123

CHAPTER 21 129

CHAPTER 22 137

CHAPTER 23 143

CHAPTER 24 151

Chapter 1

People are forgetting.

I reach back to the night. An inky line connects me to the event. I wonder how anyone can forget. If I tried to pull away the line would tighten and drag me back.

"Honestly my memories from that time are quite hazy," Lizzie tells me, snagging a miniature toast crisp topped with mackerel and cream cheese. "Do you know how many things have happened since then?"

For others, a lot, as their Instagram would attest – new jobs, first house keys, christenings, weddings – in fact we were at the latest wedding (a pre-wedding party, to be precise). Not to mention a pandemic had swept in from Europe and locked us indoors for two years, unable to fully move about in normal life for most of the year after that. People had read new things, changed belief systems, sung new songs, moved to new locations and created new milestones.

But not me.

It had been over six years, and I was still there.

On the surface of the moon.

I was also here in the glitz of Halifax's central event space, surrounded by old friends and strangers – the Bride and Groom's assorted relatives we had never met before and whom we would likely never get to know beyond a quick chat at the wedding itself on New Years Eve, after Christmas had passed.

Pinpricks of light danced around us from glimmering fairy-lights covering the bar. Sprigs of holly clawed along ancient paintings in gilded frames which hung from old-fashioned, ceiling to floor wallpaper in dark blue stripes. Severe chandeliers, all

11

angles and bulbs, added coldness to the warmth of the golden fairy light glow.

Going to a wedding when you haven't seen the people involved for two and a bit years of lockdown is a strange feeling. Are they the people you remember? Do you recall them as they were, or as they are? Memory can be tricky sometimes.

I was surprised sixty people had managed to fight their Christmas schedules to make it, though with the way the previous year had been, lockdown threats and tier systems, I suspect most were excited for any excuse to get out of the house. An event was an event! Plus, it was catered. The bride's family had money and a few years delay had boosted the wedding savings to extravagant levels.

Clearly saving for their wedding had been a far cry from the kind of scrimping and saving we had all done during our other Missing Years, nearly six years past now, in Sheffield, where the church took more than twenty percent of our income and most of our time, allowing us only part-time jobs or reliance on friends and family topping up our banks to settle our bills, while the church raked in tithes and offerings from some of the poorest families in the city. We were happy to give. As they told us, you can't out give God, one day you'll wake up and it will all have come back to you.

Looking around, perhaps they weren't wrong in that respect.

Or perhaps Christine's family, her father from Poland and mother from a wealthy family in Edinburgh, would have always paid for a gorgeous wedding and G's blessing had nothing to do with it. Even now, those thoughts feel like a betrayal of faith. What blessings would be snatched away for such lack of faith?

I was about to press my friend Lizzie on exactly what she has forgotten from our time when a commotion within the gathered clan caught my attention. Clapping hands with everyone he passed as if he had never heard of social distancing, my best friend, Dylan, pranced through the midst, grinning, laughing, slapping the groom's father on the back, winking at the waiter with the tray of canapés, until he finally emerged by my side.

He grabbed me in a side-hug, squeezing my shoulder into his chest.

"Hi Dyzzie," Lizzie smiled at him, using their old nickname (Lizzie and Dyzzie) before turning back to examine the appetizers more closely, chasing the waiter down.

Dylan murmured in my ear, "Can we get out of here yet?" He was ready for a cigarette and a walk. He was hyperactive, always ready to move on to the next thing. "Come on, can we go, can we?"

We couldn't. Not yet.

He rolled a cigarette on the reflective surface of the bar. An aggravated barman gave us an annoyed glance and then continued pouring cheap sparkling wine over orange juice to serve as over-priced Bucks Fizz. Dylan always said he could give up smoking anytime, and would never switch to a vape as it defeated the object of being rebellious.

Dylan and I stepped out through sliding doors to find ourselves on a balcony. The air was cold but clouds held back the frost.

As Dylan blew smoke into the moist air, I thought about all the times we would nip out of events at church so he could smoke, leaning against the stone of the ancient building while I would watch him, infinitely jealous. Back then, he would be on what, his third or fourth girlfriend of the year. Each one was given the blessing of the church elders, "Ahh yes, she really is the one God is setting out for you." But weeks later, when they broke up, "God's telling me to end it," she would say, maybe because she had become too attracted to him and was afraid they would end up sleeping together, the mortal sin of that time. Dylan seemed to swiftly shrug off the heartbreak. He had better dating prospects outside of our small church circle and soon settled (for six months) with the girl who ran the cafe two streets away from the church. He was shunned for dating a non-con (non-convert), but they ran well together. Maybe her anchor outside of our wild world was what kept him safe.

Most of the men had worn blazers to the pre-wedding dinner, but Dylan had on a bright yellow McKenzie hoodie. I had found a jacket and trousers which matched each other at a charity shop thrift store and called that a massive win. I didn't want to draw attention to myself as he did.

I heard the door slide open behind us and Sebastian, one of the most intelligent yet irritating people I ever met, joined us. "You two are not still canoodling outside buildings are you?"

Dylan held his cigarette between his teeth, span on the spot and expertly wrapped one arm around Sebastian's neck, ruffling his perfectly quaffed curly hair into disarray.

"Alright, alright, leave it!" Sebastian pulled away, never one to fight back. Sebastian and I shared a hug. The best part of hanging with this lot again was the amount of human contact. Pandemic be damned, we had missed that, being apart for so long. I was already on my tenth bracing hug of the evening.

"What we talking about?" Sebastian asked.

"How long it's been since Dylan went out with Lizzie," I replied with a grin. "How long did that last?"

"Two weeks?" Sebastian suggested, but Dylan answered at the same time, "Two days?"

"I swear you were dating longer."

"We had a lot of COFFEES together before she decided what God was saying was, 'Date the football captain instead'."

"That'll be it." At our church, the term 'having a coffee' meant either two attractive young people sitting down to set relationship boundaries or someone being sat down, in trouble with a small group leader. I would always have been in the second category,

Dylan in the first. I couldn't recall Sebastian sitting down for a relationship DTR (define the relationship) in that time, and he definitely was never in trouble. Perfect student.

"I forgot about him, Football Fred. Why's he not here?"

"Think he's got two kids now."

"Football Frya and Football Francis."

"And not with the person God apparently told to date him, so…"

Sebastian grimaced. "Some of you spent a lot of time not listening to what G was saying."

"Look, we tried." Dylan laughed with a shrug.

We actually did hear God, thank you very much, Sebastian, do you mind?

I held the comment inside my throat.

Besides the missing Football Fred and a few notable exceptions, there were more of us here than not here, so I shouldn't have been surprised when we went back inside to run into—

"Morgan!" Sebastian enveloped the greying husk into a hug. Dylan abruptly disappeared, but I felt trapped under the intense eyes of our former leader, surrogate father figure and former instigator of many, "Let's go for coffees," when I was in some trouble or rather. I noticed his lips curl into what could be misinterpreted as a snarl before transforming into a thin smile.

We opted for an awkward elbow bump – the recent reinvention of the handshake for modern times. "Hello, Harry, how are you?" He had certainly not forgotten what happened in our last couple of weeks before the gang broke up the final summer, never to go back.

"Good, I'm good thanks. How is St Michaels?"

The snarl-smile returned. "Very different there without you kids." I knew from stalking the church's Instagram, a complete revamp in style, presence and presentation had been instigated in the time we had all been gone. "Less…" He rolled his tongue around his mouth, seeking the right word. "…passionate, more grounded."

They had spent the last year planting trees in local neighbourhoods. Grounded was a good word, a complete diversion from our era of sky-gazing.

"Are you staying in Halifax?" I waved a hand towards the town which glowed outside the darkened windows. I was ready to switch topics, and name-dropping the town tended to be my key to unlocking a subject I can (pun not intended) go to town on. "Did you know Anne Lister is buried here and lived nearby, last summer we visited Shibden, her home."

I could flip any conversation into local queer history. Here in Halifax, Anne Lister lived from late 1700s to early 1800s with her partner Ann Walker. They even got married on Easter Sunday in a communion ceremony. As much as I love to drop this kind of information into small talk, I kicked myself for having not asked more questions about St Michaels while I had a captive audience. All day, every day, while I am around people who never knew and can't begin to understand, it is at the forefront of my mind, yet the one opportunity I have to unpack our history and the historical chat I opted for was local knowledge.

After Morgan extracted himself from our company, "Better freshen up before we eat," Sebastian glared in his direction. Did they have a falling out I didn't know about?

As we settled into our seats for food, Christine Nowak, the bride, stood up to say a few words: "Thank you all for coming, I know it's nearly Christmas, whoop whoop! But we wanted everyone to get together and remind yourselves who everyone is before the wedding. Hi, I'm Christine." Everyone chimed back like we were children in her primary school class, "Hi Christine!" We cheered and laughed as she continued.

"It has been a while, but we consider every one of you to be family, and as we are family, it is only right that we come together at Christmas and then see in the New Year together! Thank you again, and we'll see you AT THE WEDDING!"

The groom, Jeremy, was up next, to say a prayer, grace for the food. I closed my eyes and held my breath. I never pray intentionally these days, but the instinct to break into prayer remains with me at all times. I cannot remember exactly how we were supposed to be. Us, together, in prayer. Eight years ago the power in the room would have rolled through us like electric lighting, hand in hand around the tables, rising till the chandeliers shook, fairy lights humming as their power sources surged, a glow so bright it would blind the non-cons.

Now, peeking one eye open, most of the table did not have bowed heads and were fiddling awkwardly with napkins or sneakily checking their phones as Jeremy began, "Father God," no mention of Gabriel at least. "We thank you for protecting us throughout the last few years and bringing us together once again to celebrate with one another and with you. Thank you for this food, the servers and the farmers who grew it for us…"

A fluttering feeling snaked from the warmth behind my eyes, down my cheeks like an internal tear, through my shoulders and into my arms. I was afraid bolts of lighting might burst from my palms the way they used to, so I folded my hands together in my lap, opened my eyes and looked up at the plaster mouldings around the ceiling, up through the ceiling, into the low mist clouds, and almost up to --

"AMEN," chanted the table, jolting me back into my seat.

"Amen." I mumbled.

It has been a goddamn while.

Chapter 2

Dylan and I had met early in the process. He was waiting to interview at the same time as me and while I was sitting in petrified silence, he was bouncing from position to position in his seat. We had both been to a Sunday service at St Michaels after coming to the city of Sheffield, he arriving for his final year of uni (having changed universities and courses so many times he wasn't even sure it was his last year at all), and I for work, having transferred to a city branch for (what's the opposite of moving to the country for fresh air? dirty streets?) some dirty streets after having almost a complete breakdown around coming out to my family.

The front aspect of St Michaels (the apostrophe is intentionally left off on all their branding) is a traditional stone-built church, with bell tower, trees needing urgent attention from a surgeon, and tomb stones rising from the grounds. In almost direct opposition, the inside of the church has been (they called it reordered) transformed into a gorgeous open space with a couple of the original furnishings ignored in the corners and everything else new (gifted, and paid for). There was deep pile carpet, stackable chairs and a projector screen which is cranked down from the ceiling to conceal the stained glass iconic imagery of Jesus, Gabriel and (naturally) St Michael on the mountain, the bright glow of God the Father reaching towards Jesus' uplifted face while Gabriel and Michael look on.

Replacing a stunning piece of art with the plain white of a projector screen was a bold move, but certainly worth it once the band started playing and song lyrics were projected with spiralling colours and shapes pulsating behind the plain font of simplistic verses and spine-tingling choruses.

An over produced video countdown which zoomed in on door knocker numbers around the city dropping from 50 to 0 announced the enthusiastic arrival of Morgan on the (stage) alter. His lean frame was uniformed in a denim shirt, cuffs turned up once, double-denim matched with jeans and finished with a blazer in navy blue, to which the radio-mic was pinned.

"Welcome to St Michaels!"

It would turn out to be named ironically, all things considered.

Dylan and I were hunted by greeters after the service. They were trained to spot and zone in on new comers with pinpoint accuracy. Zombies with the scent of brains. We were given invites to dinner after the next service, you MUST meet this person, have you followed us on Instagram? We need to get you plugged in to a small group! Dylan had winked at me over the increasingly large crowd of friendly faces. I must have looked terrified, but my heart leapt at the sight of him.

He was freckled, wore a Hawaiian shirt and yellow shorts and had a silver chain of dogtags at the intersection of shirt buttons and skin. He seemed at ease in any crowd.

I was equal parts terrified and relieved to find him seated, knees jiggling, opposite me at the Small Group interviews a few days later, where a church leader would grill you and assign a Bible study group to match your skill-sets, personality or theology. I had been signed up for this session before I even knew what I was agreeing to, by Lizzie who had attended St Michaels forever and knew the drill.

"I hope you get it," Dylan whispered conspiringly, perched on the edge of his seat, leaning towards me.

"What?" I was surprised when he spoke. I had been quietly watching him, slack-jawed, from under my fringe for the last twenty minutes while the guy ahead of us was being chatted to within Malcolm's office.

"The role." He said, as if we were in an audition. "I hope you get it."

I could imagine him on stage, playing a knight or holding a skull above his head receipting Shakespeare in an excited chatter.

I had been feeling nervous about how I might be perceived by the church team, but Dylan's comment disarmed me. Being "saved" as a Christian wasn't a role for me, at the time. It was an identity, a personality, as true to me as being gay or tall or a complete geek for researching the history of every town I visited. I feared an interview might invalidate where I was at right now with my faith and sexuality.

I should not have worried. St Michaels was VERY inclusive, almost exclusive in their inclusively. Being a gay Christian made me a star performer right away. Being a smoker did not have the same affect for Dylan, but nonetheless we were both assigned the same small group, Skygazers, and wound up spending more and more time together.

It soon became clear that Dylan would chase any girl who crossed his path, though he had also kissed a couple of guys in college, so I heard. We were not going to date because I was far too awkward to ask him out, and he seemed oblivious to my attraction, and so we fell into an intense friendship instead.

"HARRY!"

I swerved back into the right lane with rain pelting on the windscreen, Dylan having yelped from the passenger seat as my mind was pulled back from where it felt it belonged – at St Michaels in the Past.

A truck rocked by us, raising a flood of spray across my red Nissan car. The wipers went to work, interrupting the glare of passing cars on the opposite side of the motorway.

"You know I'm a good driver," I insisted, shaking myself back to the present with a wiggle of my shoulders against the drivers' seat.

"I know you are good, and you are driving, two totally different things!" Dylan's feet were propped up as he sat, slouched low, on the passenger side. Dylan had brought pick-and-mix sweets for the journey home. I was still stuffed from the chicken supreme served with mushroom, bacon and cream sauce, followed by mounds of profiteroles lashed with chocolate, but Dylan was topping up on sugar.

"Do you think its weird people don't remember?" I asked, formulating the growing sense of unease I had felt creeping through me ever since speaking to Lizzie earlier in the evening.

"People do not WANT to remember," Dylan corrected. "Did you see the way Malcolm was watching you the entire time. Like you're a bomb and he's one of those robots sent out to defuse unexploded devices. Except it looks like he fell into a lake and got electrocuted instead. The man is frazzled."

"He's definitely changed."

"His jacket was tweed and he had PATCHES on the sleeves. Is he a farmer now?"

"I wonder why he came? If he's still so scared of us?" Because we know what happened.

Dylan fell silent for a beat, an eternity for him. "I'm telling you, Morgan is one of those disposal robots. He had to be there to check where all the bombs are now. I think most of the fuses fizzled out long ago, to be honest, maybe only yours is left, Hazzer man."

"I dunno. Sebastian still has his number for sure."

"Sebastian's is full of shit. He thinks he has everything tied up in a neat bow, but it's never that clean." Dylan placed his hands together in an upward-pointed prayer motion, and sat up straight.

The reflective glow of headlights formed a halo above his head in the windscreen. "You two canoodling out here?" he intoned, not a bad impression of the saintly Sebastian.

The goody-goody was the only one of us who had gone on to study theology, leaving St Michaels obviously, but still plugged in to the system in a way the rest of us were not.

I wonder if I would still have lost my powers if I had followed his route instead of my own. Or maybe I still had them. It's just that I never practice. For a moment I wondered whether me and Dylan would get a chance over the wedding weekend to pass the spirit from one to the other, maybe turn on a music CD from the past and see if it takes us anywhere, the way it used to. I bet he will not want to, but maybe he can be persuaded. Wasn't it fun? It was fun, right? Before.

I remembered the way others in our group had envied the connection Dylan and I carried at St Michaels. The energy we called the "Holy Spirit" practically CRACKLED between us when we were in the same line, or more powerfully, opposite each other, our small group divided into two rows, facing one another, with our hands outstretched to almost touch in the centre above our heads, forming an aisle through which we all passed one by one, breaking off from the end of the row to walk or run back through while the "spirit" fell between us.

Dylan and I had the ability to just look at each other be knocked back as if hit by an invisible force. A ball of power could burst from our wrists or eyes and knock us clean across the room, battering each other back, till we fell laughing on the floor, bent double, cackling till we couldn't breathe. Or, that's how I remembered it.

I felt my stomach flip at the memory and stole a glance off of the road toward Dylan. He was illuminated by the glow of his mobile phone. My chin suddenly tucked itself in toward my neck, jolting my whole head forward in an involuntary motion. A hiss rushed out of my lungs through my teeth.

"Bless you," Dylan said without looking up, as though I had sneezed.

My boyfriend often said the same thing, "Bless you," when I saw a crucifix and my lungs crumpled, air escaping in a WHOOSH.

I turned the indicators on and pulled off the motorway. Almost home. Almost back to my boyfriend and our puffy grey cat called Scrumples.

Chapter 3

Scrumples was waiting for us at the bottom of the stairs when we stepped into my boyfriend's house (my house too now, but his until I moved in). I closed and locked the kitchen door quietly behind us, and switched on just the low lights. Rocco would already be sound asleep. He had text me goodnight before Dylan and I left Halifax. A couple of hours in, he will have passed the snoring stage and fallen into peaceful sleep.

"Hey baby," I whispered to Scrumples, as the cat swished past my ankles, surprised by our late night entrance but excited to get midnight snacks. I shook out some crunchy cat biscuits onto the tiles.

"If you wanna brush your teeth, before you go up." I reminded Dylan where the bathroom was. "Spare room should be made up, so just make your way up when you're ready."

He had stayed before. His latest girlfriend (J-something? H-something?) lived about half-an-hour from here by train, so we have been able to welcome him on his journey a couple of times in the last few months. He would head over there tomorrow night for Christmas Eve and catch up with us again in Edinburgh for the wedding at New Years.

Leaving Scrumples and Dylan downstairs, I crept into the bedroom I share with Rocco. He was lain out across the whole bed in a diagonal, but shifted over when I slipped in beside him, stirring but not waking.

Rocco and I had met five years ago at a village fete. His village and his fete too. He was one of the organisers of the small fairground style community gathering. He had lived in this village for all twenty-seven of his years and was connected to everything and everyone.

My good friend Christine, who was now getting married, was then still living in Sheffield and would pick me up every couple of months for a drive to the countryside. We loved to explore random villages or to visit interesting locations. We had been close friends at St Michaels, and the incident didn't change that.

Especially because we never mentioned it.

The day I met Rocco, Christine had wanted to see the Scarecrow Exhibition in a small village called Tantony Edge. Boots on, we had driven into the countryside to walk around the trail. I had researched Tantony Edge ahead of our arrival and knew they exhibited scarecrows for two weeks a year in the summer and had done so for nearly fifty years. I hadn't been able to locate a notable queer hero for this particular village – even though there is always one if you know where to look. A court document. A confirmed bachelor described as somebody who loved the colour green or was said to not be able to whistle. If only we had access to them, all kinds of documents can hold a flourishing queer history. On the other hand, a farmer boy, turned gas engineer, like Rocco, may never have written about his love affair begun at the village fete and we may never read about it.

We parked up (by which I mean, abandoned Christine's Mini Electric precariously close to a ditch) at the outskirts of the village and made our way through the hedge-lined roads towards the centre, following a route which took us past the majority of the homemade horror-show of scarecrow displays.

The straw-stuffed models varied in quality and size from a GIANT Ice Cream Cone constructed from velvet and umbrellas, to a cute, tiny teddy bears' picnic with papier-mâché sandwiches peeling in the sun.

One house was fronted with an exceptionally glamorous Jill making her way up a hill (aka green sheets on ropes) with a bucket in one hand and an absolutely crushed Jack beneath her feet. Jill, a mannequin whose elegant dress was draped in luxurious purple material puffed out by net-curtain underskirts wrapped around chicken wire, had an elegant Louboutin heel on her creepy plastic foot as she stepped over the fallen Jack, the illusion only hampered by a nail hammered through the red sole to hold it in place.

Who in this Godforsaken town was extra enough to invest in such a shoe for such an event? Gazing up at the house itself, I saw the beautiful grey face of a fluffy cat peering out the front window, frozen in place as if disturbed in a private moment, one leg stuck up in the air. This was how I first met Scrumples.

The sound of steel band drums floating on the summer air drew our attention. Christine and I scurried downhill to investigate, finding ourselves at the gates of a village fete field, annexed to a tiny chapel.

The sight of any church building activated a protective response within me. I touched my thumb against the ring I wore on my left hand and it began to glow.

Closing in on a church or place linked to religion in those days, I had to shrug into my armour. My automatic reaction was to start breathing a prayer, allowing my body to be shielded with an invisible force connected to the source, spreading like light from the ring on my hand.

Though Christine did not notice, as we approached, I was mouthing a prayer which would resemble nonsense to anyone who didn't understand the intimate angelic language. "Ke a teha re ka cheteha, tala mah fategha, che phe tegah." The words ran together like someone attempting to pronounce the whole alphabet.

Abacadkimnappquadubixuez.

When I was at the Sheffield church, we had learned to draw spiritual material into the real world. Our spiritual leader, Morgan, encouraged us to have faith in the invisible protection of G.

I could feel solid forms surrounded my body. Cuffs clicked together around my wrists, expanded upwards, wrapping a gauntlet of solid protection around my sleeves, clamping shoulder pads into place to hold a breastplate. I touched my waist as I felt the belt of truth rush into place, slipping through the loopholes of my skinny jeans. Tipping back my head, I absorbed the feeling of a helmet rushing outwards from my forehead to the back on my head, a sheet of protective material extending over my eyes, blurring my vision momentarily, until I blinked myself back into the moment.

Christine was handing a couple of quid to a kindly old woman on the gate as an entrance fee. I pressed my hand against the handle of a sword which extended beside my leg. On my back, a longbow slid into place, arrows rustling together in a quiver over my right shoulder. I followed Christine into the churchyard which was filled with canopy covered stalls and families buying refreshments from a large marquee tent. They could not see my armour, but I felt safe from them, separated, removed.

I gave a weak smile to the crypt keeper at the gate and hurried after Christine.

I had been able to feel the armour surround me when it was needed, ever since a St Michaels mission trip to another church community a few years before. We had been ostensibly there to support a church in their community, though later Morgan explained the principles of these trips were to remove all the building blocks of a person before building them up again in the image of G. Far from home, out of schedule, humbling jobs, this is the work of God in us to make us new, renewed, rebuilt. We were set to work clearing gardens full of garbage from one end of a street to the other, painting walls for an elderly couple, running craft workshops for local kids and handing out flyers for a church event on our last day.

The first day of the mission trip, we had gathered in a community centre which doubled as a service space to draw the Holy Spirit down on our plans for the week. Lizzie had written up a chore list, a shopping list and a spending plan. Christine was doodling inspirational phrases on the back of paper invites to the church, interweaving them with prayers for each message to reach the right person. "Let the Light In" wasn't exactly a specialised message, and read rather more like a horoscope from the local newspaper. She added brightly coloured stickers of smiley faces and rainbows. Sebastian was searching the Scriptures, looking for a unique call to place over each of the week's events.

I was stood in the centre of the space, in silence, my hands held out in front of me, palms up, in the receiving pose. Whispers ran through my head. Over there. To the left. Behind you. I raised myself onto tiptoe, closer to G, felt him touch my outstretched hands, soft trails of dust tickling along my palms, glitter falling away through the gaps between my fingers.

Every wall of the community centre contained large windows, shuttered with blinds only half open to shelter the room from the external glare of the midday sun. Jeremy walked the exterior of the room, muttering to himself and dropping to his knees in front of each window, then rising up and pulling down the drawstring to slide the shutters fully open and let the light in. (There was that phrase again.)

I raised my arms out to each side, in the shape of the cross, sun beams to my left and right, face front, feet front, eyes front. Morgan had taught us to use our whole bodies in prayer, to lift our hands, to engage with symbols. Reaching over my shoulder, I sensed a quiver filled of arrows, and, appearing in my right hand, a longbow, sleek and cold to touch, invisible to anyone else in the room.

I pulled arrow after arrow into the ridge of the bow, against the string, fully extended and released them through the now bright, fully exposed windows. Shafts of pure gold whistled through the air, untouched by the walls, and burst across the rooftops of the town. I kept spinning in place, releasing volley after volley of arrows, spinning and spinning. As I prayed, the rest of my armour clanked into place around my spinning body for the first time, breastplate, belt, shoes, and finally the ring, slotted onto my finger as if designed and fitted especially for it.

Dylan and Oscar pulled me out of the spiral, breaking the connection by bursting through the front door of the centre with bags of groceries from Lizzie's list. "Come on lads, let's eat!" Dylan cried.

After lunch, I washed plates while Oscar dried. He was a big guy, taller than me with wide shoulders and big hands. I handed him the damp crockery and he dried them with a tea-towel.

"Where'd you get that ring?" he asked.

I thrust my palms below the washing-up-liquid bubbles, preservation instinct not allowing me to look like an idiot. Slowly I lifted my left hand free of the water, soapy suds dripping off it. "You can see it?" There was a ring around my index finger.

The ring was not made of any identifiable material. If anything, it felt more like the lack of substance, rather than substance itself, the feeling which remains when you expect to hug someone but they do not move into the hug, or you miss a step on the stairs.

"Of course I can." He smiled shyly. "It's practically glowing, and so are you."

I had been embarrassed, but secretly pleased to be given such a compliment. The water bubbled over the edges of the washing up bowl into the sink.

"I mean it," Oscar had said. "You are going to do great things."

"With Gabriel?"

"Or without."

Back on the fete field in Tantony Edge, I felt the opposite of glowing. Even though the sun was shining brightly, a shadow had formed around me along with the triggered armour. Being so close to the chapel, any church building filled me with a looming sense of impending doom. Still, I trailed after Christine as she investigated the local knitting group stall, threw ping-pong-balls into cups to win penny-sweets and posted her vote for best scarecrow into a shoebox with a hole cut in the top.

She was always self-assured, despite her losses.

Eventually, I found a fete activity to suit me. A Smash Cabinet! £1.00 would get you three wooden balls to throw at an assortment of old plates, pots and unwanted vases which were lined along the shelves of a discarded sideboard. Shards of porcelain were shattered across plastic sheeting in place to protect the grass below.

I paid my "pound for three" to a whiskery gentleman and sent the balls hurtling toward precarious china. Again and again. The cracks and crashes were satisfying as blue-painted saucers, mismatched cups and a cow-shaped teapot were sent careening off the shelf. I am not known for being aggressive, nor sporty, but permission to rain temporary destruction was too tempting to resist.

I could almost see Morgan's blurry face reflected in the painted sheen of china patterned places. "You and your friends are going to destroy us." I could hear his words echo from a previous encounter. "You were never supposed to believe that hard."

I whipped my final wooden ball like a bowler at a cricket match. It rocketed forward so fast it blew a hand-painted saucer apart and left a splintering hole all the way through the back of the wooden cabinet built to hold the game.

"Woah there." My bowling arm was arrested by a strong hand and I was broken from my reverie enough to notice a farmery lad in navy overalls who had been watching my multiple strikes against his fete's flatware. He had jumped in to intervene. "Maybe that's enough Coconut Shy for one day."

I wasn't aware of how tunnelled my vision had become until I shook my head and brought the fete field back into focus around me. Miles of colourful bunting fluttered from a turreted tent. The steel drum continued to echo around us. A hundred people from the village milled about. And, the farmer lad was stood beside me, grinning wolfishly.

As he led me away from the games stalls and through the folding flap doors of the marquee tent entrance to find a cup of tea, I couldn't say he was very impressed with my sporting prowess.

"I've been collecting crockery for months for the Smash Cabinet and you nearly went through it all in ten minutes," he told me. "I'm Rocco, what's your name? You aren't from around here are you?" Born and grown in Tantony Edge, he knew every Tom, Dick and Harry in the village. Not me though, I was a Harry from elsewhere.

We sat down at one of the fold-out tables covered in a pink paper cloth and he handed me a strong tea in a recyclable cup. I noticed his fingernails were painted the same bright red as the shoes on the Jill Scarecrow.

"It was yours!" I blurted out, putting two and two together. "The scarecrow with the Laboutin shoe!"

Rocco laughed. "I'll let you in on a secret," he says conspiratorially. "They are cheap high-heels with nail varnish on the bottom!"

"The grey cat, she's yours then?"

"They are mine. I don't want to push any gender expectations onto a cat. They're called Scrumples! Maybe you can meet them sometime?"

Two months after the fete, and multiple dates later, Rocco was sat on the edge of his bed, holding a hand out, reaching towards me. He wouldn't have seen me unclasp my invisible helmet as I undressed, or noticed as I slipped off the holster of a sword and a quiver of hidden arrows along with my t-shirt.

It was time to lay it all down.

He watched me with a look on his face as if I were a puzzle he had only just begun to understand, as if I was the most interesting thing he had ever seen.

As I reached towards him, he caught my hand and pulled me onto the bed, and as I collapsed into his arms, I let my other hand fall away from me, straightening my fingers enough for the immaterial ring to roll down past my knuckle. With a final flick of my thumb, I sent it scuttling across the carpet. As I turned my face up to meet Rocco's gaze, he kissed me softly. The ring, an image of protection I had surely only ever imagined, sank away into the carpet strands and the space where it used to live on my finger felt free.

I'm grounded.

I'm safe.

And back in the present, five years later, on Christmas Eve after my friend's pre-wedding party, I slid into bed beside the solid warmth of Rocco's body and my fingers brushed against the palm of his hand. His fingers closed around mine as he mumbled something in his sleep. I rested my cold cheek against his shoulder. I wouldn't fall asleep for a couple of hours yet.

Despite laying down my old armour, on nights when something has shaken me up, my unchecked internal self-defense systems still kick in.

TICK TICK. The electricity meter might click at an inaudible level through the daytime, but it hurts my ears at night when I am on high alert.

FLASH FLASH. The internet box illuminated the room like lightning.

Under the bed, I could hear Scrumples chew at their feet and then scurry into the hall and back and out again. They clawed at the carpet and bounced about.

The ants of anxiety always defy gravity, keeping tension in the top of my body, around my chest, the tops of my shoulders, as if they are pulling me up from the bed. Perhaps they are tied into the tides of the moon.

I turned over a few times, restless. With my eyes closed I could still feel the shape of the room, like a blueprint imprinted on the inside of my eyelids. I could see, more than feel, the sparks of adrenaline zigzagging through my arms, up and down them. My feet tapped against the bottom of the bed. I turned over again and Rocco stirred.

I was afraid I would upset him, affect his sleep and he might wake up frustrated. His slow breathing assured me he was still in deep sleep mode. The sound grated against the edge of my brain though, scuttling up and down like a long hook being dragged through my thoughts.

Creeping downstairs to sip water from the kitchen tap, like a cat, was refreshing enough to reset my mood. I told myself not to be annoyed at the night noises. I knew they were not the real source of my annoyance or fear. I wondered if Dylan was asleep. I hadn't heard him moving. It had been a long time since we shared a house or a space this closely.

Better get back into bed before I follow that thought too far.

G, let me sleep, bring your peace. G, let me sleep, bring your rest. G let me sleep.

34

It is not that I believe anymore, but the repeated words still carry weight as they used to, and draw me towards the morning.

Chapter 4

Being squashed between shoppers in an aisle of TK MAXX, arms piled high with hangers of shirts in every colour and jumpers of every description, and being pressed towards the changing rooms by your best friend on God's green earth, at lunchtime on Christmas Eve, is not The Thing, let me tell you.

Dylan had dragged me from shop to shop since we had parked up opposite the train station in Macclesfield from where he would later catch a short ride to his girlfriend's place for Christmas. We ascended Macclesfield's ancient stone 108 steps from the station to the town at a pace and he had been prodding me to "Pick a present!" ever since.

"There's nothing I need," I insisted as Dylan threw another shirt across my shoulders, this one dark blue and patterned with embroidered cherries. Wire hanger hooks poked at my body from all directions under the pile.

"It's not about needing, what do you want?" We squeezed through lines of bored partners waiting outside the changing rooms, and disappeared into one of the cubicles together. Belts, jeans, even a hat had come on in with us. Dylan divided the spoils, pulling off his coat and t-shirt to try new things on. His smooth skin flashed, and I felt a glimmer of heat remembering the crush I had on him back at St Michaels. While he was dating other people, I was dreaming of our future together, a dream of carrying the cosmic fire and electricity of the spirit to communities all over the UK, while sharing an electricity of our own.

"Try these." He handed me Fila branded tracksuit trousers and an oversized G-star Raw hoodie. "Comfy no?"

I was swimming in the soft material. "I don't know if it's...."

"Swap for these." He stepped out of grey jeans and handed them to me along with a red-check cotton shirt and an orange knitted jumper. Facing the mirror, I loved the combination of the popped collar and the thick stitched orange wool. I really look like myself. Instantly I wanted to take it off.

Dylan caught my eye in the mirror, his head plopping free of a Jack Jones sweatshirt. As if he sensing my thoughts, he interjected, "You are allowed to look good, you know, to feel good."

I was not sure. Any moment in which I felt most alive, most myself, most in touch with my humanity, I wanted to cringe myself into non-existence.

"Mate, you don't think you deserve anything because we were taught that our bodies are not worth anything. You remember what Morgan used to say, if you love something, give it up. They told us to turn off our favourite music, to donate our best jumpers, and to only keep enough cash to make it through the week, IF that." He broke into an impression of our mentor. "Whoever has two coats, give one away, and make it the good one." Dylan's face was full of kindness, but his eyes darted furiously, angry at the teaching we had been fed week after week at St Michaels. "Remember when you came to morning prayers with new trainers, they were comfy, slick, and you had saved up for them. Morgan called you to the front of the room and told everyone you were an example of someone making their body an idol."

I had been quick to leap to my feet when Morgan called me forward, always excited to be involved in an illustration or to answer questions when called upon at morning prayers or small group. Morgan had asked me to the front of the room, indicated for me to step up onto a chair. I wondered if I were going to be asked to give the blessing, to hold my hands wide above the group and rain down glory over them.

Instead, Morgan grabbed my feet, breaking into the popular social media phrase, "What are thoooose!" Embarrassment flooded up my body from feet to face. "In the kingdom of heaven, we do not prioritise style or comfort for our feet, we prioritise stepping in time with spirit! Be aware of the cost of living for yourself, of living for your body, of living in comfortable shoes. They say you have to walk a mile in someone else's shoes before you can understand them. I say, you need to walk someone to God who is the only one that can understand them. You cannot understand your needs in this world, but you will receive everything you need in the world to come."

Dylan continued speaking, interrupting my memories, as he gathered all the clothing together in our changing room. "You were told not to make your body an idol, to empty yourself of every desire and to be filled with G from the soles of your feet to the top of your head, but life isn't like that. You deserve good things for yourself, for now, for this moment, for this life. Look at you, confident, stylish and fit as anything. Your body deserves to be cared for. You deserve to be cared for!" Realising he had begun to preach, Dylan switched to a crowing voice and he declared loudly for everyone in the changing rooms to hear, "IT'S CHRISTMAS EVE AND YOU DESERVE LOVE!"

At the cashier desk, Dylan insisted the shop assistant wrap up my clothes with colourful tissue paper before placing them into the bag. He settled the bill with his credit card and handed me the handles of the bag victoriously. "Merry Christmas, my friend!" pulling me into a hug smack dab in the middle of everyone else hurrying through their last minute Christmas Eve purchases.

Chapter 5

Scrumples was waiting for me on return to the house. They don't meow. They just make little beeping sounds like an electric car backing into a parking space. If you give them a gentle poke in the belly with the right timing, they might even be able to beep along to a tune.

"Meep meep!" the cat squeaked as I squeezed through the door caught between two huge bags of groceries, a last minute attempt to fill up on Christmassy snacks, nibbles and cheese.

I hadn't noticed when I got in last night, but Rocco had spent the night before putting up Christmas decorations while I was away at my friends' wedding party. He worked for a gas company and was on call all the way up to Christmas and had not been able to come with me to the event yesterday. Obviously making the most of his time without me, he had strung tinsel from every corner of the house. Strings of iridescent colour crisscrossed the ceilings, dangled from the banister and flowed across the mantelpiece above the fireplace in our living room. Gold, silver and every gaudy shade you can image gleamed and bobbed, rustling gently around me.

Scrumples had managed to catch at least one string and demolished it at the foot of the stairs. I swept up the shredded remains into a dustpan before unpacking my food supplies into cupboards.

Wandering the supermarket in a daze, I had attempted to follow Dylan's advice to listen to my body, to treat myself with dignity and desire. Discounted chocolate oranges had piled up in the shopping cart.

I set about preparing a Christmas Eve dinner.

Miniature new potatoes were dusted with olive oil and Maldon sea-salt and roasted in the oven. Carrots drizzled with hot butter, mustard and honey. Leeks were bathed in a cheese sauce whisked from home-made roux and three types of grated cheese. Pigs-in-Blankets crisped in the oven, streaky bacon coiled around chipolata sausages pierced with spikes of Rosemary. Sizzling oil and meat juices were tipped from the roast pan into gravy, thickened to pour. Slices of succulent, lamb, cooked pink.

Christmas songs piped from the radio when Rocco arrived home from work. On Christmas Eve he always spray-dyed his hair blue, a tradition he had started as a joke on having a Blue Christmas the year before he met me, but it had become a yearly staple and everyone who worked with him expected it for the last days work of the year.

Dinner was served, the fire set, and an evening of Christmas Eve bliss was had. Soft kisses by the fire-place. Countdown to Santa's arrival.

Look, that was the plan.

Instead, Rocco walked in, blue hair and bright smile, to be greeted by scenes of a disaster and it all started when the archangel Gabriel showed up.

Tipping the boiling new potatoes into a colander, steam billowed. The softened mini potatoes hissed as they hit hot oil in a baking tray. I had made it through the process of chopping, cleaning and preparing all the vegetables in peace with Christmas tunes accompanying my unhurried actions. But as everything cooked with different times, temperatures and expectations, I began to feel my panic rising. Could I make a perfect meal?

Heat blasted out the open oven door as I slid the tray of potatoes inside. On the hob, carrots boiled uncontrollably, adding to the haze of steam and heat filling the room. As water bubbled over the edge of the pan and hissed against the electric hob top, I sensed a presence, moving, above me.

Emerging from one of the spotlights on the ceiling, each individual, bony, clawed finger at a time, like a spider returning up

42

from a bathplug after you've washed it away, two strong arms pushed free from the lamp in the ceiling and crawled towards me, dragging their body out behind them as I turned, horrified from the stove.

Grey dust trickled onto the floor tiles as the creature moved above me, popping through bands of tinsel, snapping the tape that held it up. Ribbons of tinsel fell around me and the angel lowered itself until his elongated feet were stood on the floor. Almost human, but with pale skin covered in cracks and caked in dust, the angelic being was taller than me at full height. His gigantic wings creaked open wide.

Though he had a round head and eyes, there was no mouth, and the words he used seemed to come from deep within me. "You will fail."

It had been years since I last saw him this closely. I was frozen in place and could not reach for my weapons because I had long since given them up. If I fight, I will fail.

The angel drew closer, his head swinging widely to the left and right, searching every surface in the room and finishing up with his face inches from my own. I could feel the vacuum of ice cold that surrounds him brushing against my cheeks. "You do not deserve good things." The voice was back. "You can never be truly filled with joy. You give glory to yourself and not to God. You are faithless. It is because of you, your friend is dead."

The door burst open and a cheery Rocco erupted through. "Jingle Jingle! Merry---huh?"

I didn't know how much time had passed. Strings of tinsel hung from the ceiling, the carrots had boiled dry, spirals of smoke coughed from the corners of the oven door and there were empty pans and knives and plastic pots of peelings everywhere. I was crouched in the corner of the kitchen, my head in my hands.

"Harry, what? Are you okay?" Rocco crossed the room in one bound, tucking his arms around me. "What were you trying to do?"

"I failed."

Rocco kissed me on the top of my head and was up again, swiping the cindered potatoes out of the oven and slinging the whole tray out into the garden where it could smoke to its hearts content without setting off the fire-alarm, dropping the inedible lamb into the sink and switching on the water. Apparently I had left the plastic wrap on. The whole thing was moments from turning into a burnt sacrifice. Soggy carrots were swiftly re-homed in the bin, along with their peelings. Next, he was up on a step-ladder, sticking tinsel back to the ceiling. "Tape never works well with tinsel! The steam must have unstuck it all! Don't worry, its fine, its fine." As he moved with grace, sweeping, cleaning, wiping, he never stopped reassuring me that everything was okay.

"I was just gunna cook us something simple tonight anyway." He slid a couple of frozen pizza boxes out of the freezer. "You didn't have to go to all that trouble. It's the Ghost of Christmas Past, not the Roast of Christmas Past!"

Eventually, I began to smile and laugh at myself for having been so ridiculous as to attempt something so huge, with no forward planning, on Christmas Eve. Rocco scooped up Scrumples and dumped them into my arms. "Look how much Scrumples loves you," he said, though to be honest the cat did not look impressed and attempted to escape immediately.

Later, when the pizzas were cooked and we were settled in front of the fire with a Christmas Special episode of a quiz show playing on TV, I could convince myself I didn't see Gabriel here in our home today, and had simply tried to do too much too soon, but when I looked at my phone, I had six missed calls from Sebastian and there was a text message that said: "He wants u back."

Chapter 6

We walked towards Midnight Mass in silence. It had taken me a couple of hours to pull myself back together. Slices of gooey-cheese covered pizza had helped. Rocco strode alongside me as we made our way a short walk from the house where we lived together to the chapel at the centre of the town, the same place we had first met on the fete field, and where an eleven o'clock evening service would lead us directly into the magical start of Christmas as the hands on the clock passed twelve.

The night was airy, cold but not yet frosty. A few blown clouds hid the stars, which peeked between holes in the sky. It was not the right conditions for snow. Not yet. A white Christmas was off the cards.

The Midnight Mass would follow the tradition of Nine Lessons and Carols, a Christmas service whose origins trace back to the Victorian Era, to former Archbishop of Canterbury, Edward Benson, whose wife, esteemed lesbian Mary Benson, was one of my favourite historical queer figures. Mary was groomed and married to Edward very young, growing into her love of women over time as she learnt how to respect her own needs and desires. When Edward died, Mary moved in with Lucy Tait and they formed a home together up until Mary's death in 1918.

The Nine Lessons and Carols service was conceived to keep local Cornish men out of the pub on Christmas Eve and is of necessity overly long and drawn out. The vicars, from Edward Benson all the way to our current vicar James Howard, run the service from the front of church, alternating between nine carols and nine readings from the ancient texts of the Bible, telling the story of Jesus birth but incorporating the whole account from the creation of the Earth through to angelic announcements and shepherds and allsorts, culminating in Jesus being born on

Christmas Day (back in the year dot, over 2000 years ago.) Carol followed by reading, carol, reading, etc.

After moving in with Rocco, I had to consistently remind myself that my experiences at St Michaels and his experience of a village church were miles apart from one another. Here, the closest they get to a religious experience was saying, "Oh my God..." when the local gossip reached a salacious moment. Congregants did not carry their religiosity within them like white noise which surrounds everything they do, every decision they make. Instead, their spirituality was folded neatly into the church building itself like the blankets wrapping the plastic doll infant (Jesus) which would later be carried down the aisle between the pews and placed into the life-size manger.

I can manage to force myself into church life (aka community life) if I find historic links between our activities here and those of our queer ancestors. I find that link helps, because it reaches so far into the past it completely leaps over my experiences six years ago.

St Michaels is a short blip in a timeline of my life and the lives of LGBTQI+ folk who came before us and will come after us.

And yet, because Rocco seems to be part of ALL of the committees, I am consistently pressed against the life of the "church" here. I have spent much of the five years we have been together adjusting my ability to share space with (to me) the dangerous shape of CHURCH, a term far too broad for me to associate every element of it with the utterly wild presentation of church I was a part of before.

The bones of Tantony Edge Chapel may technically be the same organisation as St Michaels, but the flesh filling them out is made of entirely different stuff.

For a start, St Michaels had replaced its traditional meeting space with modern branding, technology, bright paintwork and comfy seating, while the Tantony chapel maintained a pew-lined, old oak attitude and whitewashed walls.

On a human level, those at St Michaels were in competition with one another to read the most, pray the loudest and to give the most. I found it difficult to bend myself out of that shape. If it were just a matter of completing the work, Lizzie would have taken home all the prizes. But on the matter of applying the work, Oscar, Sebastian and I were considered to be on another league.

At the chapel here, I am known as little more than Rocco's boyfriend, a presentation I have made effective use of in order to stay safe, for now. The less involved I am, the less I can be exposed or hurt.

I scanned the room, estimating the best seating position to attract the least attention. Sitting at the back would set off alarm-bells, but too close to the front suggested the kind of a self-importance which finds a person signed up to the volunteering lists within a few weeks of attendance. Rocco had disappeared immediately to speak to others from committees and church organisations, so I slipped into a midway pew, alone, and nodded hello to a few friendly, wrinkled faces surrounding me.

Looking around, I took in the carved wooden statues of the "holy family" which loomed from the front of the church, held in place with a length of chain and a padlock disguised by folds of white silk printed with red berries. Beyond the stained wood of Mary and Joseph, the altar (table) is laid for communion with a silver serving dish of wafers and a holy-grail cup for wine. One of the fiercest locals was fussing with four purple and one pink candle. The purple had been lit week by week through Advent, and tonight the pink candle's wick would be set aflame as Jesus arrived at Midnight.

I smiled at their naivety (and at their nativity). We had been taught it very differently at St Michaels. Jesus, if he existed, would not have any power here until first light.

There was a lesser light to rule the night.

The organ creaked to life while I flicked through a pamphlet of ancient hymns to find the lyrics and liturgy (not unlike unwrapping the case of a Britney CD to find the song words in the days before Spotify). As the service began, the vicar processed down the central aisle with a plastic doll wrapped in blankets to be laid in the manger. I remembered Morgan blowing out the purple candles one by one as Sebastian dutifully carried an armful of wrapped cloths toward the alter in St Michaels, the dramatic stage lighting lowering with every step and sinking the entire church into darkness as our unique Christmas ritual began. A drum beat which had been holding steady with our heartbeats sped up in the darkness, increasing the sense of expectation and anxiety among us.

Back here, Rocco sidled into the pew beside me and clutched my hand, leaning against me to peek at my hymn sheet as the first song led us into the service.

Later, the vicar opened a Bible to speak the "word of the Lord" (thanks be to God.)

"In the beginning..." The vicar spoke, but I could hear only Morgan's voice, echoing from the past. "God created the heavens and the earth..." Rocco was between me and the exit of this pew. If I had to leave, I could not get out without causing a scene. I gripped his hand tightly as the vicar continued. "God made two great lights – a greater light to govern the day, and a lesser light to rule the night."

At St Michaels, we had been shrouded with darkness when these Bible verses were read aloud. We were still just about able to pick out the figure of Sebastian stood before the altar. As the chorus finished and the lights came back up, we could sense something was wrong. He had not tucked Baby Jesus into the cradle, instead, he turned slowly and reverently towards us and dropped the folded cloths open, unrolling white silk to reveal no doll, only empty material.

Looming above him, separating Sebastian from the alter, caught in the growing glow of stage lighting, was a majestic creature, with six-foot wings stretched out wide either side, casting a shadow from the stage out across all of us as we gawped from the congregation, our jaws hanging open.

Backlit, with sparkling robes, this angel announced: "Do not be afraid!"

The angel was just our friend Oscar. We all sat back in relief. He had carefully decorated silver-foil wings and a ring-light halo. His over enunciated words were the performance of a lifetime. "Behold, I have good news for you, a message that will fill everyone with great joy!" Oscar did not know then, this would be his last Christmas.

Now, I was desperate to escape the church I was in, but politeness insisted I stay, caught up in a whirlwind of carols, readings, standing and sitting as commanded, then shaking hands (tapping elbows in some cases), greeting everyone with a Merry Christmas and a "have a good new year", before Rocco and I could get out shortly after midnight.

As we exited the chapel, as if on cue, the clouds parted above the village, revealing a glistening full moon.

Chapter 7

Scrumples was not the least bit interested in their Christmas Stocking.

I had filled the knitted sock with colourful packets of treats, their favourite cat nibbles and toys. If I bodily lifted them off the nest they'd made out of a blanket on the sofa, and dropped them feet first onto the stocking, it was possible they may stay long enough for a quick photograph to be captioned, "Scrumple Clause." But equally they might squirm away.

I scooped them up for a big kiss on the head and set the cat free to scurry back to their nest.

Message received, Scrumps.

Santa Claws Do NOT Stop Here.

I loved Christmas, so no amount of grumpy kitty behaviour was going to stop my effort to enjoy Christmas this year.

Rocco was dressed and ready to go by the time I had finished fussing with Scrumples. I could see he was dressed moderately, having washed all the blue out of his hair from the night before. He paired beige chinos with brown shoes and was scrubbed up in a plain white shirt. At least he did not have a tie on—wait, yup, there it was, currently wrapped around his hand. It would be knotted in place before we got to his moms' house, and I would have to call him Richard for the day.

Rocco's moms met when he was five, his having been born into the previous marriage of his biological mom, Brenda and wannabe rockstar Frank. Brenda's current partner, Jennifer, moved to Tantony Edge after they met at a small-business networking event in Leeds. Rocco's dad, Frank, would join us for Christmas Dinner later. He had never remarried and remained fully involved in his son's life after the marriage broke down, even living intermittently in the house with his ex-wife and Jennifer between gigs and tours as a guitar player. Now, he lived about twenty minutes drive away in the nearest big town, Macclesfield, in a rented flat.

You might assume a family which had been forerunners of progressive dynamics in family structure would carry such progressive views into every area of their life, however, in their case a small-to-medium-business attitude prevailed over unique structure and they presented themselves for the most part as traditionalists, supporters of Conservative politics on every other point. Brenda and Jennifer may well have voted for Tony Blair and new Labour, but would definitely have switched right back when minimum wage increases were on the line in recent elections. I would never dare ask which way they leaned on Brexit. That debate had apparently never reached Tantony, or had been laid to rest before I arrived. Their 3D-Printing art business had been able to continue unimpeded during the pandemic, once minimum-wage workers were allowed to return to site.

I try not to follow all of the ins and outs of the progressive vs traditional in their house. All I know is Rocco becomes Richard the moment he steps through the door.

Richard is lovely and all, but a little more stayed than the person who wore a knitted "Smash the Patriarchy" Christmas jumper with jingle-bells sewn at nipple height to his workplace Christmas Party.

Jennifer is all teeth. She embraced us in the doorway with the kind of smile which announces from television screens that 9 out of 10 dentists recommend this brand of toothpaste.

Brenda had hot chocolate simmering on the stove-top and cook-from-frozen croissants growing into puffed-up pastries in the oven. We would be expecting more and more guests before the day was out. Boots constantly stomped on the doormat, announcing arrivals. Scarves and coats were swung over the banister as the neighbours, neighbours' parents and neighbours' parents' neighbours all poured into the house throughout the morning, draping themselves all over the lounge furniture.

In the front room, a huge pine Christmas tree reached from the floor to the ceiling where a giant star-shaped topper tapped against wooden panelling. Rows of bushy branches were adorned with 3D-printed ornaments from previous years' collections. Hanging by silver threads were plastic Post Boxes in a variety of gaudy colours and imitation stamps which boasted faces of Queen Elizabeth II from the many eras of her reign.

Having bought a house next to a dairy farm in the village, Rocco's moms had developed a close friendship with their nearest neighbours, a farming couple. Traditionally, the farmer and his wife (and their assorted relatives) flooded into Brenda and Jennifer's for a welcoming Christmas morning drink and pastries, before going back to the farm. Rocco's earliest memories were helping bring cows in from the fields to be milked and he was a proper farmer-boy in his teens, working with the neighbours until he studied a trade at college and eventually took a job fixing gas boilers in his twenties. The family's shared Christmas tradition had started when Rocco was little and continued every year as though nothing had changed. Clutching mugs of hot cocoa, young and old perched all over the long green sofa and matching armchairs in front of the tree.

These were not my people. I bubbled with Christmas excitement, but you would not have known it to see me stood beside one of the armchairs, sipping at the super sweet cocoa. I had never known exactly how to interact with this crowd. I was not given a rule book upon joining the family. I still could not understand the in-jokes and hadn't studied up enough to find out.

Every now and then I attempted to interject with an interesting story, but it always came out too strong.

At a previous family buffet over the Easter weekend, I had suddenly launched into the tale of Anne Lister and Ann Walker being married by taking communion together in 1834. I hadn't meant to burst in so abruptly. The farmer was talking about a wedding they were attending in the summer so I thought it seemed the right moment to expound a tale of queer romance, but everyone stared at me as if I had thrown a glove down on the table and demanded a duel. Brenda and Jennifer, who had not openly fought for gay marriage and once it was available, had chosen to simply change their last names to match and brought life insurance that would ensure their company, house and inheritance would pass to one another, had awkwardly sipped their tea. The village may have been open to lesbian and gay relationships, but replacing traditional institutions like marriage with queer versions was considered a taboo subject. "So this wedding is in July?" Rocco's dad had diplomatically switched the subject back and everyone carried on without me.

In my time at St Michaels, one of my roles had been volunteering at a small group, under Morgan's directorship. At the Skygazers evening once a week, students and young adults brought food to share, read a Bible story aloud and we chatted about methods to apply the principles of the story to each of our lives. Before dinner, we would each state the best and worst thing we had done that week. We knew each others secret battles, personal feelings (and failings) and external circumstances better than anyone. Whenever a new person joined our small group, each of us would ensure we spoke to them individually, asking about their family history, their connection to God, the movies and TV-shows they loved or hated, and which subjects they were studying at university. We would never have let one of them arrive and spend the evening, let alone five years, feeling like an outsider.

Of course we also took their money and gave it to the church, reduced their confidence and personality and encouraged greater and greater dependency on the group itself, rather than individuality. But I digress.

I love Christmas.

Even from the corner, I could feel the glow of the family's happiness. Cheeky comments rang out as they pulled open presents. I was not very good at buying presents for other people, so provided a lot of biscuits in novelty tins from me to the farmers and farmers' relatives. "A biscuit tin shaped like a Scotty Dog! How imaginative!" one of them exclaimed, unwrapping. "It will go well with the Polar Bear tin from last year!" But did I detect a side-eye between the farmer and his wife?

Brenda and Jennifer gifted everyone ornaments from their latest 3D-printed collection. This year it was snow-boots in a variety of red, white and blue patterns, which, on some, looked suspiciously like a Union Jack.

I tried to style my face to seem grateful, but not too grateful. I did not want to look either ungrateful or spoiled. Unwittingly, I thought about Dylan's speech in the changing rooms about deserving nice things. I didn't want anyone here to imagine I thought I DESERVED nice Christmas presents. The thought of Dylan's speech, or maybe his closeness, flushed my face as I opened packets of socks, a quiz-book I am guaranteed to never fill in and a packet of Lady Gaga branded pink Oreos. Actually, those were pretty awesome. I waggled the packet at Jennifer with a thankful nod. She looked relieved to have picked out something I liked. She quite literally breathed a sigh of relief and shared a smile with Brenda across the coffee table.

Was I so difficult to be around?

Someone had bought me an Anne Lister calendar, with pictures from the TV series based on her life. My face, already flushed, deepened to a purplish red at the overcorrection. Had my little outburst of a story at Easter stayed with them so much they felt the need to buy something branded to placate me? I felt embarrassed.

Conspicuous by their absence were any cards or presents from my own parents. Quietly but forcefully Christian throughout my childhood, my parents had been unlikely to react well to my coming out as gay in my late teens. My mum and dad had met at a Youth Camp for pastor's children and had been heavily influenced into thinking LGBT people were dangerous servants of Satan who would destroy the traditional family unit. I waited as long I could to come out to them, but it had to happen one day or I would never be able to date openly. Eventually, on my twentieth birthday I wrote them a letter, and phoned on the day they received it. A flaming row had left us not speaking ever since.

I joined St Michaels only a few months later – running away from my old life. Unlike my parents, Morgan welcomed me as a diverse member of the family of God. "We've been waiting to have a few gays on the team for some time!" he had announced loudly when we first met. As volunteers, we were encouraged not to date at all, so we could give more time to serving God, but that was true for the straight team as well as the gay team. Come to mention it, the straight team did seem to be on dates all the time, but only when they felt God had specifically called them to go out with one another, which was all the time.

I touched my tongue to the dried cinnamon powder stuck to the rim of the hot chocolate mug. This tasted like Christmas to me. The rip of wrapping paper sounded like Christmas. The scent of pine rising from the tree each time someone dove under to pull out gifts smelt like Christmas. Christmas is still magic, even if your body is screaming to escape.

When the presents were nearly all unwrapped, I sat down beside Rocco on the coach. He handed me a cardboard box, which had been left at his workplace, but with my name on it. He had picked it up on Christmas Eve when he was at the Macclesfield depot dropping off his van for the break. "This arrived for you!"

I assumed it was something he had ordered online. Usually, he did all of his Christmas shopping in one night in late December, staying up until two in the morning on Amazon, working through a list of names.

I undid the tape and drew out a dark blue gift box covered in gold stars. "For me?"

I removed the lid and tipped the contents onto my lap. Falling from inside the box was a heavy ornament made of solid porcelain, surrounded in bubble-wrap. I twisted it free, spinning the object out of its protective layers onto my knees.

A delicate design, with hand-painted, picked out wings and robes and a raised halo, staring up at me was a luxury, ornamental Angel Gabriel. The sight of him took me by surprise and I gasped, standing up and letting the figurine drop out of my lap onto the lacquered wood floor.

The angel smashed into a dozen pieces.

Chapter 8

"Don't you find it frustrating?" I asked Rocco as he set the table for Christmas lunch with the best cutlery. I indicated the house with a wave. "Not being all of you when we are here? I mean, you're wearing a tie. And you look very cute in it, by the way." I reached for the knot of his tie but he ducked out of my grasp.

"You don't have to be everything, all the time," he said, shutting the drawer in an oak dresser while searching for placemats. He handed me the mats printed with Christmas trees.

"Is it not very...it's not very, honest?" It was probably (read: definitely) not the time to get into it, but I couldn't help but notice the ways he was less Rocco and more Richard when he was here.

Once I had come out, there was something in me which snapped and I now found it extremely difficult to deal with people who were not being fully open. I know that presentation is not all you are, but when someone usually wears multiple bracelets and hoop-earrings on the day-to-day and isn't camp as Christmas actually AT Christmas, it breaks my heart a little. "As long as you are being yourself, I love you whatever you are wearing." I looked him up and down. "Or not wearing."

He gave me a little twirl like he was at the end of a runway. Ahh there he is. He leaned over to give me a kiss on the cheek. "And I love you when you are chucking your mysterious angel on the floor, and generally being mysterious, so I guess we are even."

It did feel disingenuous to suggest Rocco was not being himself, when I was not exactly rushing to reveal all my superpowers to his family. Do I even have superpowers anymore? I haven't checked for a while. In an emergency, surely, but maybe I should –

Lunch interrupted further discussion, as Brenda and Frank brought out endless dishes of prepared vegetables -- roast potatoes, brussel sprouts mixed with chestnuts, green beans, mashed potatoes, and a root vegetable pie for Frank and Jennifer who are both vegetarian, along with a plate of sliced turkey for Rocco, Brenda and me. Honestly the pie, which oozed butter and a creamy sauce when cut into, looked as good as the turkey and we helped ourselves to a little of everything we fancied.

Later, Frank and I gathered all the wrapping paper and bits of packaging from the lounge into rubbish sacks. It was traditional for us to take it to end of the garden and to set a small bonfire in the afternoon, while Brenda and Jennifer fell asleep in front of the TV and Rocco did the washing up. As Frank set up twigs into a pyramid over a fire-lighter and twisted paper strips into a rusty fire pit, I shook the wrapping paper, ribbons and various small boxes onto the grass.

Frank never said a lot. When he did talk, it was in a low tone which gave his words gravitas. "It can be hard for you without your family at Christmas," he said to me, between blowing on the sparks, more of a statement than a question.

I tried to shrug it off, laughingly, "Oh, I'm fine, you know me!" as I handed him a handful of balled up wrapping paper to touch to the slowly growing flames.

"Richard's moms and I, we don't know everything that happened with the angel Church thing. Richard tells us a few things about it. I know it affected you a lot…" He paused, unsure if he had said not enough or too much.

I was surprised he was so aware of my history.

"People don't always understand the fullness of a life they haven't lived," Frank went on, gently feeding more fuel into the fire. "When Richard's mom and I broke up, and yet kept living together, and Jennifer moved in, there were people talking about us, not understanding our choices, but that's life I'm afraid. You don't always get to see the whole story." I had never heard him open up like this. He went on, "I hope you know you are part of our family story now."

I had always lost my families. My biological parents had disowned me. St Michaels was the next family and look at them now. Still, I felt he meant it kindly and tried to nod meaningfully even though I wouldn't accept it as a truth for me. I was my own family at this point. Me and sometimes Rocco. And sometimes Dylan. The rest...

I picked up the last few bits of card and paper from the lawn and handed them across, including the starry blue box I had been mysteriously sent. As Frank took the box from my hands, a cream envelope slid free and plopped down onto the grass.

Whoever sent the angel figurine had sent a letter too. Ripping it open, I knew who.

Chapter 9

The heat of the train dissipated rapidly as I disembarked at Manchester station and aimed towards a queer-owned coffee shop across the bridge, down a few steps and an alleyway into the Gay Quarter. I knew a few good spots here, although I had never spent much time on Canal Street, despite the location being one of the most famous LGBTQI+ safe spaces, filled with nightclubs, karaoke joints and eateries pressed along the canal, with high fences preventing anyone from tipping into the water after celebrating too hard during Manchester Pride.

Opposite the bars and cafes, a peaceful park provided refuge from the noise of the city. Sackville Gardens was made of green lawns and metallic art. At the heart of the park, a sculpture bench gave passers-by an opportunity to sit and commune with a statue of Alan Turing, the well-known code cracker from World War II who was tortured for being a man who loved men at a time being so was considered illegal. He passed away with an apple half eaten beside his bed. Very Adam and Eve. Very father of us all.

I wondered, gazing through the chain-link fence across the water into the park, whether he might be able to crack the mystery of the files I had been sent on Christmas Day. Instead, I roped in Lizzie to help me.

Alan Turing is not my favourite Manchester queer icon, which has to go to Harry Stokes, who died in 1859 and led a very ordinary life as a bricklayer, business owner and trans man. It is only because we have access to court documents, firstly from a divorce and later from newspaper rumours after he died, we are aware he existed as an ancestor in local transgender history. No one lives in a bubble. He must have had his own struggles without being able to talk to people around him, to seek advice or to trust even some of the people closest to him. He appears to be someone who knew who he was and how he wanted to present himself to the world. I wonder if not being able to speak about it left him awake at night filled with anxiety, repeating sentences over and over in his head, having entire conversations with an audience that was never truly there.

"Happy Christmas, darling!" Lizzie emerged in front of me from the fog which hung about the canal. She wore a pinstriped party-suit under a camel-skin jacket with a scarf so enormous it was only out-larged by the size of her bag which I knew would contain a wealth of useful items for our quest. "Let's get inside."

In retrospect, I should have picked up a Christmas present for her since I think that is the rule within the Eve/Day/Boxing window if you see friends. Instead, I promised to pay for drinks. I had insisted on our meeting right away! Cappuccino for me, Irish Coffee for her.

"Time doesn't exist over Christmas, might as well get started early!"

Out from her Mary Poppins' bag came notebooks, pens, an ipad, a bulldog clip full of papers and a Ziplock bag of home-made Mince Pies. She waved away the waiter before he could be bothered by her illicit pastries. "Show me what you've got and I'll share what I dug up after you called yesterday." She shot me a pursed lip to say I should have known not to call her mid-afternoon on Christmas day. But I wasn't wrong, she did have a bunch of the files I needed and probably some of the answers too.

"I'm sorry for dragging you back into it, but you have to admit Sebastian is taking it a bit far, posting creepy dolls to Rocco's work?" The broken angel figure had gone straight into the bin and by the time I found the envelope and realised who must have sent it, we were too late to pick the pieces back out from amongst the remains of a big roast, so I had to explain its haunting presence to Lizzie rather than bringing it with me.

"Very Sebastian to go too far, though."

He was the only one of us who had stayed in that world when the rest had got out. He had moved away, but dove headfirst into Bible school. Most of us had put our Bibles back on the shelf, if not lost them altogether, after the incident. From conversations, I knew a few still found comfort in traditions of faith, but each had forged very different paths. Sebastian's was a round road which took him right back to the start.

The printouts I had been sent in a cream envelope were accounts from the three years our group of friends had primarily spent at St Michaels. Lizzie had worked in admin at the church, volunteering two days and paid one. She had easily switched into working as a professional personal assistant after leaving.

As I laid out the files, she explained these account details were accessible online for organisations registered as a business. I had always assumed the church was a charity but it had been a Limited Company all along.

The accounts were broken down across multiple complicated looking sheets of tables with descriptions in-between. One table on each had been circled in red pen, the annual payment figures of the trustees. I was stunned. While we were volunteering every free hour we had, Morgan had been pocketing £70,000 a year taxable income with a £30,000 house payment. £90,000 paid off his house in 3 years. £210,000 income.

And he was not the only one. Among the "grown-ups" we remembered being his friends, always gathered close to him at church but never seen doing the "jobs", many were signed onto the organisation as trustees and received chunky house payments, hefty love "gifts", and incomes for "consultancy".

Lizzie and I assumed Sebastian had sent me this information following our run-in with Morgan at the party on Christmas Eve eve. He could have just WhatsApp'ed it instead of including the delicate (and creepy) angel decoration to get my attention. Mind you, it had worked.

"Seventy grand might not seem a scandalous amount to some people." Lizzie shared her thoughts, shuffling through the papers and jotting notes into a lined pad. "But many folk in our congregation were living off of the Food Bank."

"Most in our group were students," I added. "Or starting out after uni. First jobs don't pay much, plus we were told to tithe twenty percent minimum."

"Minimum!" Lizzie echoed.

Morgan would boast from the front of church of his own time at uni, giving us a spiel, "God never let me go hungry. I had a box a cereal which never seemed to run out, poured bowl after bowl for weeks! You cannot out-give God. When I was at university like you lot are, I would give thirty percent of my earnings to the church, and it was as if God tripled my blessings for doing so, tripled my grades! I always had A's and I spent as much time praying as studying back then."

I tapped the documents. "Is Sebastian trying to hint Morgan was corrupt the whole time?"

"More than hint, we already know Morgan was playing a dangerous game with us, teaching something he did not believe, but the idea he was dragging money out of our purses and popping it into his mortgage? I'm furious." She bit into a mince pie. Juice burst out and down her chin, so she dapped at it with a paper napkin.

"You were working for the church directly." I waved away a mince pie, then changed my mind and napped one. "I was volunteering at small group, and doing set up on Sundays. Christine was on cleaning duty for six months, while penning her dissertation." All the jobs we took with the understanding that God and G required our outward as well as inward devotion.

We were not the only ones working for free. The Food Bank was fuelled entirely on volunteer hours. Various Small Groups had been encouraged to start projects such as gardening for local homes in exchange for a small donation to the church. We were told these projects would build a family spirit between us and that G would work his way out in the world via our hands and our feet.

"Gabriel cannot leave the darkness," Morgan would preach, his words building toward a fever pitch, "but you can! You can push a lawnmower in the light and pray the blessing of Gabriel over the grass as you go. You can carry Gabriel with you to paint a fence, leaving his presence in the houses you help out. We can transform this town and release Gabriel by doing in the daylight the tasks he asks of us in the dark."

"Trust me, I know." One of Lizzie's roles had been linking local needs with church volunteers. There had been a whole spreadsheet of congregants' skill sets. "And more." Her growing annoyance was waking up a specific set of memories she had moved from short-term to long-term memory. Now she was bringing them back to the forefront of her mind and was becoming steadily more agitated. "Morgan had a pin-board in his inner office with every name on it and their secret shames. It was usually covered over with a cloth, but I occasionally glimpsed it."

Small group leaders would feedback to the top team any concerns about members gleaned from the shared stories over food. I thought about the times I had taken notes during the sharing of our "best and worst thing we did this week." I had often fed these notes directly back to Morgan, never putting together all the connections.

Lizzie nodded furiously. "Yes, and he would get on the phone with people who did not offer to volunteer and wear them down. He would tell them, 'G can see your pride. You might not see it yourself, but there is a pride growing within you which is bordering on a danger to your salvation, it's a block to your receiving the joy of G's blessing. We have an opportunity to wash cars in town this weekend, which will help you reduce pride into humility. I would not ask it of you, but G wants only good things for you.'" Her Morgan impression was a whine, but convincing enough.

"And all that time, the donations were filling up his bank account, and his friends?"

"All above board." She waved the accounts. "If the charity commission examined these, chances are they would agree with the consultancy fees!"

I shook my head. Everything we had put into that organisation was dust.

"And that's not all." Lizzie undid the papers from the bulldog clip, slapping them down onto the table. "He kept a file on every one of us."

My head was baffled. It felt like opening the door from a steamed up bathroom and magically stepping right out into a pile of snow in Narnia. Clarity pulled fuzzy edges into sharp focus. I felt the betrayal sharply and it should have hurt more. I was used to numbing those memories, so having someone sit down and say, "Here are some facts about your past" was such a sharp shock I couldn't quite process the injury.

After the incident, we had all sensed with horror the harm St Michaels ran on, hidden by outlets of kindness such as housing a food bank for those in need, but none of us had been aware of how deep it had run, or how intentional it must have been. Was it modern-day slavery? Morgan's blessings from G had been bought and signed for by our hard work and offerings.

I still had to cycle back to something Lizzie had said; that Morgan never believed but in the meantime --

The thud and collapse of paperwork scattering all ways across the table drew me from my thoughts as I scooped paperwork away from the edges and prevented our drinks from getting knocked over. Lizzie tapped her empty glass, "Can I get another?"

"What are these?"

"I copied all of the files with names I recognised, in case we ever needed them, after...you know, the incident."

I did.

"Morgan had them in a drawer. I photocopied them while he was talking to the police, before I got out of there."

Each file had one of our names printed in bold type at the top, our address at the time, details of employment, medical files (how did he get hold of these?), a family tree, details of our dating life (mine, blank, Dylan's extensive).

"We shouldn't go through all these." I admitted it would be wrong to read too much, even though it was tempting. "Didn't you date Dylan at one point?"

"Ha Ha. Didn't YOU date Dylan at one point?"

"No. Definitely not!"

"Definitely not also!" Lizzie's freshened drink arrived, a welcome interruption. "Look at this section," she thumbed through one of the files. "Spiritual Gifts."

Prophecy. Healing. Transportation.

Speaking angelic language. I felt the rumble of syllables pulse through my bones, as if crawling up the ladder of my ribs one by one to emerge instantaneously, but I shut my mouth to it and swallowed the sounds back down.

"He had us all listed by what we believed we could do," Lizzie said, and she flipped back to the beginning of the file. "He was planning to move us into new locations, to extend the brand. He was looking for true believers. See? Three files stamped TB for True Believer. Yours, Seb's and Oscar's."

I rubbed my thumb over the copied ink stamp. The original paperwork has been embossed where the rubber and ink had been pressed down tightly. Oscar, Sebastian and I were rubberstamped to be the new leaders? It made sense. Morgan was always talking about an expansion and asking who we would put on our leadership team when the opportunity arose.

The first couple of years, Morgan had focused on Sheffield in his sermons, but as time crept forward, he had begun to speak about The North. He had projected an image of the Angel of the North monument onto the screen at the front of church and declared it a sign of the higher counties being won in G's name. "Manchester, Leicester, Leeds." He had been planting seeds of new powerhouses to emerge from his "brand" of Christianity.

Now she had started, Lizzie couldn't seem to stop. These were stories and ideas that had festered within her since the incident, since she had worked it all out. She had not been able to explain it to anyone else. Who would have understood at the time what she meant? It wasn't until I sent her photos of the documents Sebastian had sent me that she was reminded of the corruption and Morgan's original expansion plan. Even when she had originally understood his intention, she had assumed he meant it for good, so that the Food Banks and Small Groups could be expanded across the Northeast, but now she understood it as a cynical cash grab instead.

A pyramid scheme of faith.

Her words continued to bubble out. "The most absurd thing is that it was entirely made up!"

Chapter 10

Lizzie looked at her smart watch and began to gather all the paperwork back into neat piles. "I have a spread to get to," she said. She was beginning to remerge from her presentation of the past and to refocus on the present. We had both gained a lot of clarity by sharing our theories on Morgan's motivation.

Mysteries had their fuzzy edges shaved off. Too much solving the past can leave your present feeling dissolved though. I felt wiped out. I had been running into the same walls for years. Finally breaking through, I found no gravity on the other side, afloat. After years of not winning, a win can feel like a loss. It's disorientating.

Another thing weighed heavily on my mind – were the incredible things we saw and did unbelievable, or entirely unreal?

Humungous bag filled back up, Lizzie lent forward and placed her hand on my arm. "Let's visit him before I go?"

He was only a few tram stops away, in Eccles. I had not been to visit in a while.

Outside, the mist had lifted (literally, not metaphorically) but the day was still grey.

We left the canal behind and picked our way through the city toward the nearest tram stop. Lizzie pulled some antibacterial wipes out of her bag to clean the seats when we got on. The pandemic had left us all with different methods of feeling safe in public spaces. When we were sat together, I returned to a conversation we had skipped over before.

"You said Morgan didn't believe his own teaching. What did you mean?"

Lizzie folded her wet-wipes inside out into a plastic baggie and stuffed it into her bag, then began to explain, as if invited to give a lecture. She had her slides at the ready (metaphorically, not literally). "It was branding, wasn't it? All of it. Morgan needed a theory of Christianity he could brand as his own. Christianity is always being rebranded. About every forty years the whole system changes. Did you know, in the early 1900s, there were streams of Christanity laser focused on maintaining white supremacy by any means, and a bunch of proof texts were dragged out of context to 'protect' against interracial marriage." She made air quotes. "Preachers and politicians greased each others palms with arguments that backed one another up. In America, being anti-segregation was considered anti-church. But as new, inclusive theories popped up, known as Liberation theory, some Christians, racial minorities and feminists were rising together against the classic structures."

I didn't know Lizzie had such a strong handle on church history, but it made sense if this liberation theory crossed over with feminism and anti-racism. Lizzie always dove into very specific rabbit-holes of knowledge and, as a Black woman, she understood history through a lens I was not always aware of as a white man. After leaving mainstream Christianity, she had found new outlets for social change. "Being Anti-Black was supposedly going out of fashion in churches, so denominations picked up a new cause, being anti-abortion and fighting for the so-called traditional family at home. The racism never left, but it went underground. They fronted with new family values language."

I had grown up within a Christian tradition which had been virulently anti-gay and threatened by trans identities. My parents had bought into this apparently "traditional" church theology which said my existence as a gay man was a threat to "family values." By comparison, St Michaels had seemed so refreshing with its inclusion.

"Every era of western church has had its unique branding, from Henry VIII launching an attack on the Catholic Church, to the crusades, to raising money for the missionaries going abroad and colonising cultures, to raising money for so-called pro-life, then raising money to fight against, you know, the gays and stuff. This is just the latest in a long trend of rebuilding church in a unique and very fundable form."

I followed her line of thinking. In order to stay relevant, new enemies had to be built up every few decades. But St Michaels hadn't created a specific enemy to fight against. I interrupted Lizzie to ask, "Who is the latest then?"

"For us, it was subtle. It was everyone!" Lizzie announced this with a flourish. "The Non-Converts. Morgan created such a distinct umbrella identity within our church that everyone else was a total alien to us. We had miracles we could never explain to them. Even other Christians didn't believe in our G, they didn't follow the same understanding of God that we did. Imagine if St Michaels had expanded the way Morgan wanted? The inside and outside would have grown exponentially."

My eyebrows were furrowed. "Sure, but we had…" I lowered my voice. Being on the tram was a very public place for such a discussion, though no one was paying attention to us. A middle-aged man was reading the Metro. A teenage couple were holding hands and sharing a pair of earphones to listen to music. Speaking quietly to disguise the absurdity of our history so that these, others, on the tram couldn't hear something they would not understand aligned with Lizzie's understanding of us vs them. The others would never understand us. Non-Cons became the default enemy.

"But we had real miracles." I hissed.

A video reel of moments fluttered across my mind, projecting images against the inside of my head. A loaf of bread, torn before communion. Sweating palms lifted skyward. Lightning passing between Dylan and me as we prayed, a glow reverberating down the skin of our outstretched arms. My hands cupped either side of Christine's face, looking deep into her eyes and speaking her future in words I believed at the time came directly from G to prophesy a partner at St Michaels was going to be in her life forever. She had glanced momentarily at Oscar. In another memory, Jeremy and I stood in the rain outside St Michaels first thing one Sunday morning calling for the clouds to move away, to leave, to shift across the sky. Our whole gang ate a picnic the same Sunday under a cloudless sky.

I remembered running, so fast, shifting effortlessly at great speed from street to street in Sheffield, one minute outside the City Hall and moments later skidding to a stop near the Cathedral.

"Did we?" Lizzie pressed the red button to stop the tram and we got up to wait near the door.

"Of course we did. You remember when our food increased to include everyone who arrived at Small Group no matter how much we cooked."

"What if we just made enough for everyone we invited?"

We exited the tram, but didn't move off the stop while we continued this discussion.

"How often did we pray for people to be healed?" Every service. Morgan finished each sermon with a call to action. He used to say G wanted to heal anyone who was here, to come forward with any ailments from a common cold to a broken leg. G's presence had anointed us. Morgan would encourage us to gather around and pray for those who had come forward. Oscar, Sebastian and I would touch the hurting part of a person and pray aloud, "Headache be gone. Have faith in the power of Gabriel. May the light of the night brighten your body!"

"Did you see anyone get healed though?" Lizzie's eyes flashed. It was clear she was hurt by my questioning the way she understood and remembered what had happened at St Michaels.

Those who had limped to the front often limped away, it was true. But as Morgan explained, it took faith to be healed. If your faith wavered, your healing would not come. People claimed their headaches had left them! Someone had seen a broken leg literally grow out, I remembered them saying so. And there were extreme stories too.

One evening, the presence had been particularly heavy. You could feel the power in the very atmosphere of the church. Morgan had invited an elderly wheelchair user to the front of the church, assisted by her grown-up daughter. "Can these old bones rise?" Morgan had cried, quoting the Bible from a story of skeletons pulling on flesh and joining a war. "Can we have two strong lads down here. Oscar, you're strong, come on down. Sebastian too." I had been about to volunteer, but he waved me away. "Get an arm under her shoulders, each of you," Morgan had instructed, kneeling before the small but faith-filled woman in her chair. Dipping a finger into a bag of grey powder, Morgan drew a line above each of her eyebrows, like wings painted across her forehead. "Feel his wings beneath you and RISE!" he cried. Sebastian and Oscar lent an arm and a shoulder to the women, helping her gently but firmly to her feet.

Her sandals touched the floor as she pressed her weight onto one foot and then the other. Her muscles were weakened from years of not walking far. As small as she looked, she weighed heavily against Sebastian, whose face gave the impression he was more responsible for holding her upright than the wings of Gabriel. Together, the three figures stepped out across the stage, one short step after the other, right to left in full view of the congregation.

A low cheer began at the front of the church and rumbled backwards through the rows, clapping and shouting, whooping, hoorays and hallelujahs, "Come on!"s and "He can do it!" (Not she can.) As we watched with our own eyes, this elderly woman literally stepped out in faith, rising from her chair to walk in front of us. "Can these old bones walk?" Morgan shouted, joining the din.

Later, we had seen her daughter, cheeks tear-stained with joy (or something else?), pushing her mother from the building in her wheelchair and using a motorised disabled ramp to lift her into the side entrance of a van specially designed to transport her mother more easily from the nursing home to visit the outside world.

As I shared this story, Lizzie stopped me. "Harry, will you shut up? Don't you know it is actually gross to use disabled people as a sermon prop," she said. "I shouldn't have to explain to you, many people who use wheelchairs can walk short distances and move about. The chair is a tool, not a burden. Hefting an old woman out of the security of her chair to parade her in front of an audience is not evidence of a miracle. If churches want the deaf to hear, they are better off paying for an interpreter to sign the sermon, not a supernatural team to try and pray the deaf away."

She was right.

"Everything we thought we saw, we didn't see. Do you understand?"

I did understand her point of view. And yet, I had felt G's supernatural power. Hadn't I? The same power had thrown us to the floor at times, and at others, lifted us toward the sky. You cannot dismiss those experiences just because you have become the outsider, gone back to being a non-con. An uneasy silence settled between us. Was I an unbeliever too? The more I tried to find a specific event or example, the less I could locate one.

And yet, here we were, at the gates of the cemetery where Oscar lay buried. And the reality of G's power, or our belief in it, was real enough to have killed him.

Chapter 11

Mossy green grass wound through the cemetery between trees with wide hips marking the passage of time. Weeds bloomed, faded, and grew again year after year along the edge of the path. Lizzie and I made our way in silence, an uneasy peace formed between us after our argument on the way here. Freshly swept gravel crunched gently beneath our feet. We could see a couple of other visitors bringing flowers.

We should have stopped for flowers before we got on the tram, I berated myself. Perhaps we can leave a mince pie, at least.

Some older graves looked neglected, their visitors no longer free to come as often as they would like, or having joined their partners, friends or family years ago. More recent graves had been left little gifts, ceramic reminders they were on their family's mind at Christmas. A gaudy, colourful Christmas kitten has been left beside a headstone, its painted paw reaching towards the cold granite. I thought about how much Rocco's moms would have appreciated the bright print of the kitten and with its red and green striped bow.

In a few European countries, families and friends visit cemeteries on Christmas Eve with jars of candles. I had never understood why you would tinge the magic of Christmas with the sorrow of loss, but walking in here today, I could sense the spirits holding vigil over the festive season.

Victorians shared ghost stories at Christmas around the fire. If Halloween was a time for monsters, so Christmas was a season for ghosts. The ghosts of past, present and future felt connected in a place like this at a time when the boundaries between the real and imaged were thinned.

It had been a while since either of us visited Oscar's grave, so it took a bit of to and fro-ing before Lizzie and I could orientate ourselves. Our previous conversation was forgotten and Lizzie's bubbly, always helpful role had returned. "I distinctly remember we passed this cross, and this eagle…" As if consulting a map, Lizzie strode down the main path and out across the soft grass between headstones. "Over here!"

She pointed down a row. Halfway along, we saw a figure in a big coat suddenly rise up, startled, to peer at us from beneath a deep hood. They were stood over the plot we remembered as Oscar's grave, and seeing us approach, they took off, making a wild dash for the exit at the far side of the cemetery.

For a moment I was too surprised at the erratic display to react, then I sprang into action. "Oy!" I shouted at the receding figure, as though Oscar belonged to us, exclusively. I set off in pursuit.

"Is that Sebastian?" I heard Lizzie shout the question as I zipped after the person in black, who zig-zagged through the graveyard like Pacman chasing coloured dots, dipping left and right through the grave markers as I made chase. They did not slow down and when they reached the gate they gripped the top and launched themselves over onto the path the other side.

As I arrived, out of breath, to lean on the gate, whoever it was had disappeared towards town. If it was one of Oscar's family, why run away when disturbed? If it was Sebastian, surely he would have stayed to talk with us?

Goosebumps ran up my back. The hairs on the back of my neck stood on end. For a moment I felt as though someone was looming above me, dust pouring down my spine, a faceless angel reaching clawed, skeletal fingers around my neck.

Lizzie interrupted.

"Harry, look!"

I sprinted back to the grave as Lizzie lifted a painted-glass, Christmas-tree-decoration angel from off of the headstone.

"Bastard!" It was unlike Lizzie to swear. "Why would he bring this here? Here of all places?"

A card had been left under the decoration, on top of the headstone. Tacky font declared, "Happy Christmas" above a fearsome looking snowman with coal for eyes and a wonky smile.

Inside, a handwritten note.

"Oscar, please, please can we end it this year."

Chapter 12

If Christmas Eve Eve (the 23rd December) contains a diluted version of the magic and anticipation of Christmas Eve, then Boxing Day's Boxing Day (the 27th December) contains an increased sense of the disappointment and "it's over"ness Boxing Day is made of.

For a start, no one is clear on what day it is. Is it a weekend? Is it a normal weekday? Sometimes the extended bank holiday falls here. Sometimes we are expected to go back to our regular activities. The sugar high is dropping. You cannot be totally sure if you are hungry or tired or grumpy or just not in the mood.

This was how I felt on the 27th December. I was in an in-between space. A pause.

In many ways, my life had felt on pause ever since the incident at St Michaels six years ago. After a major trauma, it can be hard to know where to go next. It feels absurd to go about your ordinary life, yet the rest of the world does not stop when you do. Bills still have to be paid. Friends' birthdays have to be celebrated. Food has to be made in order to survive, if not for enjoyment. After some months, or years, you may begin to forget that you are only living to survive and you form new patterns, find new things you enjoy, and create new memories.

But other times, it can still feel like you are waiting. Waiting for the other shoe to drop. Christmas celebrations have come to a grating stop but the promise of New Year is not quite here.

In this way, I could understand, partly, the motivation for a request to Oscar's spirit to, "end it this year" from the same person who sent me those financial files on St Michaels. Our history had been hanging above us for so many years without closure.

I certainly did not appreciate their methods, but I had to agree with the card-sender's message. It was time to settle it.

If Lizzie was right about everything having been false, it was time for us to grow up.

On the occasions I have tried to talk about my experiences with Outsiders, Non-Cons, from my work or in the village, they have often given me an incomprehensive gaze and nodded along, "I'm sure you were very young and naive back then." But having faith has nothing to do with being young or old.

I knew that having faith or believing in Supernatural or unrealistic things had nothing to do with age or maturity. When we were part of St Michaels our group of friends had considered ourselves the Youngsters, partly because we were treated that way, but also because Morgan and his circle of close leaders were in their fifties, while we were mostly late teens or early twenties. The congregation was made up of a range of ages, while about sixty percent were students or young adults, there were a middle group of families with young kids, and a top row of what we called the Grown Ups, who had professional jobs; Lawyers, Doctors, Business Owners and among them Morgan the ringleader.

If Morgan was the Captain of the St Michaels ship, then his Number 1, second-in-command, was a man called Doctor Barnabas. I recognised his name referenced a number of times in the financial documents as a consultant, and remembered he was taking a chunk of cash out of the church each year as a £9,500 payment towards his "housing", invested into his own mortgage. Whether the good doctor bought into Morgan's faith theory about the angels, or whether he was brought in by Morgan's cash payments was unclear, but being a part of the organisation had nothing to do with being young or old. Anyone could be taken in.

I wondered if Dr Barnabas was the reason our medical files were stapled into the information packets held about myself and my friends, which Lizzie had copied for us. With a blush of pride, I remembered my file stamped with TB – true believer, and having been picked as a future leader. Morgan had seen something special within me. Or had he seen someone with no connections, who was easily manipulated.

On Boxing Day's Boxing Day, Rocco had left me with Scrumples at the house while he visited his moms to put together a buffet. They were having extended family (yes more, but their own aunts and uncles, not neighbours this time) for tea. I was planning to join them later, which gave me plenty of time to curl up on the sofa with Scrumples and consider my past, present and future.

If, as Lizzie proposed, the past was made up, the present with all of its apprehension and the feeling one day we would be pulled back into the craziness, wasn't real and isn't necessary. Like the Christmas card left at Oscar's grave suggested: we could end it this year and step with renewed purpose into the new.

Lizzie's philosophy of our shared history did not acknowledge the source of our trauma though.

Oscar had died that night and only we knew why.

Or did we? Maybe there was more I could do to find out.

"Off you get," I told Scrumps as I stretched to my feet forcing the cat to hop off. They dashed away as soon as they landed, disappearing up the stairs.

I checked the time on my phone. Rocco and his family were not expecting me to join them at the house till about five, so I had a couple of hours to enact my plan.

Going back to that place.

I never thought I would, and yet here I was, forty-five minutes later, getting out of the car Rocco and I shared when he didn't have his van over the holidays. I was parked on the road outside St Michaels in Sheffield. The place had not changed much, but the signage was different. Posters for their Christmas Services had not been taken down yet, the imagery showing starlight streaming onto a stable scene and instead of Mary, Joseph and the animals gathered around baby Jesus' crib, cartoon trees were bringing gifts in their boughs, trunks bowed or kneeling beside the manger.

St Michaels is set back from the road, surrounded by ancient graves. The stone brick building doesn't extend a natural welcome, and yet it used to be a hive of activity. When we attended on a Sunday, the grounds were crowded with groups of friends and students chatting, laughing, and Dylan smoking, outside before the service.

This year, the grass had been left to grow tall, picked out around the edges with bamboo sticks and netting to stop people wandering off the path. A six-foot, plastic, printed banner suggested the church was intent on preserving wildlife and celebrating the bees with the slogan: "God's World. Let it Bee."

Good for the environment as it may "bee" it was hard for me not to see all this as a new, cynical, trendy brand instigated by an enigmatic leader. The netting, an entrapment for a new youth culture which cares about the Earth more than Heaven, who once drawn in would be bled dry of money, time, energy and left with scars for years to come.

Tall grass was bent from the rain and wind of winter and clung damply around flat, historic gravestones. Under the netting, under the grass, was the unforgiving ground where Oscar had been found dead in the early hours of the morning six years ago.

I shuddered at the thought of him laying out there all night while the rest of us hurried home, shaken from our shared experience in the church hall.

Returning brought with it an eerie feeling of the past on repeat. But I was here to secure our future. I pushed on up the path towards the tall front doors.

On week days, the church is usually left open for locals to enter so they can spend time in prayer, or at least it was in our day. I had not considered what to do next if it was locked, but as I shook and rattled the wrought iron door handle, the door itself wouldn't budge. Damn. Locked.

I peeked up at the creepy face of a carved gargoyle grimacing from above me. "What are you looking at?" I stuck out my tongue at the creature.

Retreating to consider my options, I took in the whole looming building, a big square of old brick with slate roof and a short clock tower at the front. The left side of the building blended seamlessly into a modern concrete and glass extension filled with offices, an updated kitchen and new toilets. I remembered there were a few other entrances around the back, but those doors were protected with security keypad locks.

Couldn't hurt to have a look.

The back of the original church building contained a decorative arch which reached towards the roof and beneath it a wide window of stained glass, depicting a pasty-faced white Jesus along with two angels, holding up his arms, on the top of a mountain. One angel was St Michael, after whom the church was named. This warrior angel was referred to in the Christian Bible from time to time, and in mythology most commonly linked to the planet Mars, another warrior. The other angel, or archangel, was Gabriel, a fearsome creature around whom Morgan had based his entire brand of theology.

I remembered Morgan's first sermon about Gabriel, who was described as being mystically linked with the moon. "Who do you think is being spoken about in these opening verses from Genesis when God establishes the order of the universe? 'For He created a greater light to rule the day, and a lesser light to rule the night.' Jesus is that great light, like the sun, too bright to approach, too holy for human contact. And Gabriel is the lesser light, made only a little higher than mankind. As it says in the Psalm 8, 'He has made you a little lower than the angels.' This angelic light of the night is ours to grasp, in our reach. Have we not sent a man to the moon? Can we not carry it with us into the day? Everybody put your hands in the air and reach for the light!"

But now, Gabriel's entire stained glass face was missing from the artwork. Something (someone?) had shattered the glass from his neck up. A halo remained, above shards of jagged, coloured glass which daggered outward from the missing piece where his cherubic face had once shone. Not unlike the creature itself, whose eyes were empty holes dragging you in, no features, wings creaking wide, dust raining down…

My hands trembled.

I crouched, pressing my palms against the pebbles of the path, feeling each round rock and the sharp edges against my skin. I was here. I was now. I was not back in that moment, facing him again. I felt the presence of my thick coat around my shoulders, the wool of my scarf, the tightness of a bobble hat.

The church wall fell back into focus as I stood up, feeling a little dizzy.

It occurred to me, the window must have been broken only recently. Someone had smashed Gabriel out of it. The window had not been fixed or patched with plastic screening. Surely the Christmas committee would not have left the broken window for all to see at the service only two days ago?

Enough about windows. I was looking for a door.

The furthest part of the newer element of the building had an entrance with a keypad lock and CCTV. Morgan had always said everything here belonged to all of us. The building, the offerings, were the property of the whole family of God. Realistically none of us had the deeds though, only he did.

As volunteers, we would come and go on various tasks and to numerous meetings, so each of us had access to the building via the keypad. What was the code back then? ANGEL. 2, 6, 4, 3, 5. I tried this combination and pressed X.

A single red light indicated the code was wrong.

"Not angel," I muttered to myself. The church had rebranded since those days.

I knew from occasionally tuning in to sermons live-streamed on YouTube, Morgan did not refer to the lesser light that ruled the night anymore, He was trying to keep his congregation fully grounded in reality. His new brand focused on an earth based theology.

I tried the numbers for "E.A.R.T.H." Red flash, twice this time.

Something egotistical, perhaps. "M.O.R.G.A.N." Three red flashes. I had a feeling any more incorrect guesses might result in my being locked out for good.

I walked back around to the front of the church where I had a burst of inspiration.

Sprinting back, I input, "2.3.3.7." Green light, click.

The door opened for the "BEES."

Chapter 13

Walking into the church offices was a daily part of my old routine. It felt both natural and surreal to be revisiting those feelings. It had been a while. We used to gather here for prayer sessions most days when we were volunteering, a mix of us, but always Sebastian, Oscar and me. I remembered Morgan teaching us to pray in the angelic language. "Allow the syllables to bubble out of you." Ke sha he rath ta kumma she la ta.

My tongue would sometimes twist into the sounds even now, especially if I felt stressed or anxious. Repeated diphthong sounds with surprise consonants. You could never be one hundred percent sure the words you were saying were an expression of the mood you were in and not an ancient curse or call.

All the hallways here were decorated in dull colours. Nothing bright. It was designed to ground you on earth as you thought about heaven. Or at least, that is how I understood the colour tones. Advertisements for upcoming events and services were pinned to boards along the corridors. I wondered who still attended from our era, and wished I could let them know they were following a fraudster who was quite literally banking on their beliefs.

Speaking of Morgan, his office was up ahead, with a slider switched to "Out." Empty.

I turned the doorknob. Thankfully it was unlocked, far too trusting for an organisation which had recently had a rock thrown through their stained glass.

Chairs, a desk, a giant pin-board covered in members' names with Post-it notes stuck beside them. Everything was familiar, and yet changed. What if he had thrown out the old files by now? I used my phone as a torch, the natural light of the winter sun slowly dimming outside the office windows.

Desk, computers, cabinets. I pulled drawers open and slammed them closed. Stationary rattled in one. Another held organisational diaries and paperwork for appointments and meetings. I dug through a pile of future talk outlines, leading from Christmas to Easter.

I sat on a leather backed swivel chair and spun in place.

I had been spinning in place for years.

Back to work, the metal filing-cabinet drawers creaked and banged as I opened and closed them, flicking through green folders of licensing, external bookings and accounts. Ah ha!

Here in the bottom drawer, right at the back, packed away and untouched for years, files with our names on. Lizzie, Harry, Sebastian, Oscar. I unclipped Oscar's personal file and slid it out of the drawer, crouching down beside the desk.

On the first page was a photo of my old friend, taken from his Facebook profile. Captured on camera, he looked his usual goofy self and was mugging off the photographer. He was never fully comfortable with his appearance and with the way he took up space in every room. He was theatrical in public, but wanted to be private and unobserved in private. He had a booming voice, even when he tried to whisper jokes to friends during church services. Despite the discomfort at being photographed, I recognised the joy within him which I had always known. He carried warmth with him, pockets full of it. His hugs were legendary. Proper Santa hugs with arms wrapped fully around you as he laughed into the top of your head.

I could not believe we had lost him.

Hurriedly, I skipped through files about his flaws, family and powers, until I found the final two pages of the folder, stapled together. There was a photocopy of his death certificate, and notes by a doctor who had answered questions at the inquest into Oscar's death. These notes should never have become public. I had a feeling I knew who had smuggled them out of the medical system: Dr Barnabas.

Through the frosted glass door, I noticed a corridor light switch on, then a closer light, flooding the office.

SHIT! I was going to be found here.

I yanked the stapled pages free of the file, folded them up and shoved them in my pocket, throwing the rest of Oscar's details back into the drawer and shutting it quickly. As I heard footsteps approach and the sound of someone talking on the phone, I scrambled into the footwell of the desk, pulling my knees inside, under my coat, just moments before the door to the office swung open.

I saw a pair of smart shoes enter the room and heard a murmur of conversation coming through the phone. The owner of the polished shoes trudged past the desk across to the same cabinet I had just closed. Whoever it was did not open the bottom drawer, so didn't see Oscar's papers sprawling across the top of the other files.

When he spoke, his voice was distinct and clipped. Morgan. "I thought he was here too. On Christmas day, after the service, after everyone had gone home, I saw him. He was so large and so present. He filled the whole height of the church. Frightened me, terrified me. But he's not real." He sounded as though he was convincing himself as much as the person on the other end of the phone.

The other voice interrupted, protested. A high pitch bubble of phone babble.

The shoes squeaked around the desk as Morgan argued. "You cannot bring back something that was never there! You kids did enough damage trying to release him when you were here. " The voice interrupted again, and Morgan began to lose his cool. "I'm not responsible for what you lot chose to believe. Whatever you unleashed was on you. Can you leave it where it was?"

A drawer was opened, diary removed, and pages turned. "Listen, Sebastian, I'm canceling all my plans to come to the wedding myself. Speak to me before you do anything stupid. But if you ARE going to do this, let me record it for my Podcast?"

The drawer closed and Morgan carried the diary out of the room, still talking. "Maybe we can combine the two brands..."

As the door swung shut behind him, I let out a breath.

It was time to go.

I crept out the office and down the corridor. I could hear him closing doors ahead of me and only moved forward each time he had walked away. Darkness engulfed the hallway. I counted to a hundred to give Morgan time to leave the grounds before scurrying down the stairs and letting myself out of the back door. The automated locks beeped back into place behind me.

I glanced up at the broken image of Gabriel as I passed. The stained glass was inky now without the sun. Turning away, I fully bumped into a shadowy figure.

"Hey, hi, wait, what?" Morgan was shocked to see me there. I hadn't set foot on the grounds in years, but here I was lurking in the dark. "Harry? What are you doing here?" He had just hung up on Sebastian and it must have seemed as though old students were popping out of the woodwork.

I stepped back and gave him an awkward wave. "Er...hi Morgan. Happy Christmas and things."

"Happy Christmas to you." He was still confused. "What are you doing here?"

"I...er..." The folded up papers in my pocket were jutting into my thigh, screaming out as stolen goods. "I come to visit Oscar sometimes," I lied. "Not that he's here. I know where he is, but I come here."

Morgan considered my face quizzically, as if he were about to demand some kind of proof. He sighed instead. "Tragedy," he said, resigned. "A tragedy."

"Yeah, the worst." I didn't ask why if it was such a tragedy, he had gone poking into Oscar's affairs and kept a copy of his death certificate secured in his office. I had not yet studied the details of the report into his death.

"What happened to Gabriel?" I nodded towards the broken window.

Morgan looked up at the jagged edge of the cracked glass, then suddenly, as if possessed, grabbed my wrist and hissed at me. "Don't mess with him. It's enough what Sebastian is doing. You can't see something that isn't there."

"You've been seeing him?" Also, what is Sebastian doing?

Morgan shook his head, releasing me. "Sebastian has. He thinks he is called to release him again. After everything, you know, everything, we stopped talking about him for a while." Morgan forced his fearful frown away. It was replaced with his usual plastic smile. "We aren't about that, Harry. We are focused on the earth now. You would love what I teach about the world we live in. Green grass. Blue sky. You'd love it."

Finally, after all the years I had known him, he looked pathetic to me.

I was amazed any of us had followed him, listened to his teaching or tried to imitate his life as our own. I shrugged passed him and started back towards my car. Morgan called out as I walked away:

"Will you subscribe to my Podcast?"

Chapter 14

Rocco was NOT pleased.

I had arrived home late yesterday, over an hour after I was supposed to meet his family at his moms' house. By the time I was changed and ready, it was nearer seven than five. He thought I did not care enough about sharing time with his family. I tried to explain about Oscar, about wanting to find out, but he told me, "You are living in the past!" The present was here, with him, with his family. The past, I couldn't even be sure of, so why live there?

I was trying to live in the moment. I was attempting to pull myself forward into this place, with this family, in this house, but something seemed to stretch me backwards like elastic was attached to my shoulders and knees, dragging me into history even as I scrabbled to hold onto the present.

Rocco did not understand time in this way. He thought about his needs and wants for today. Yesterdays problems evaporated faster than the morning mist. Hungry? He would make a sandwich and not dwell on it any further. Sleepy? Go to bed. Horny? Well.

Not like me. I ruminated on every decision, scared I might make the wrong one, worried something I said, or did or didn't do might haunt me forever, again.

I could not formulate the right series of words to explain exactly how I had come to be so late and instead spent the evening chastising myself while nibbling on Brenda's cold beetroot bombs and nutty, root-vegetable-paste crowned vol-au-vents. Rocco was right. I had been late. I did not want to direct my annoyance at him, so I aimed it at myself. What was I thinking? I sat chiding my behaviour all night.

In the morning, with a bowl of Coco Pops crackling quietly into mush in a bowl in front of me and Oscar's files unfolded on the table in the lounge at home, I did know what I was thinking. I had gone back to Sheffield for a reason and it was to do the bidding of the message left on Oscar's grave: Put an end to it.

I could not fully understand the wording on the death certificate, but I could make out most of the details when combined with the notes a doctor had typed up to present his explanation of the death to the coroner at the inquest. The case had aroused some attention due to this young man being found dead in a graveyard outside of a well-known church with no easily apparent cause of death, in the early hours of a Thursday morning.

Considering we had seen him die, we should have known before the news presenters did. Or maybe we did not see anything. The memory doesn't fit the narrative now. It's blurry.

The inquest report gave horrifying details. His tongue was dry, as if all saliva had evaporated before he died, or as he died. This was noted as a bizarre, unexplained factor. Cause of death was listed as asphyxiation, suffocation from loss of breath. He would have lost consciousness from loss of oxygen to the brain. His lungs were ruptured, shredded, but still in place, bone dry, all liquid evaporated and gone from them, as though pulled out.

As for the rest of his body, he was entirely covered in bruising. There was severe tissue damage below the skin, the space around his joints heavily swollen. The doctor could not present an explanation for the damage, suggesting the young man seemed severely bruised, as if dropped from a great height.

The doctor indicated the damage was most consistent with being suddenly evacuated from a plane. Lack of oxygen from the pressure difference, bruising from impact. However, no bones were broken. There was swelling around joints and below the skin, but no breakages from a heavy impact. Internal organs, besides the lungs, were undamaged save from increased blood-pressure causing strain on the heart in the last few minutes before death.

We had not known these details at the time, only that Oscar had been found at St Michaels the morning after our prayer session.

While the police were interviewing Morgan, Lizzie had hurriedly copied all of our files. Before the end of the day, I had told everyone I was leaving town. We were all scared of what we had seen. Morgan tried to bury the whole thing. The rest of us went on to pretend nothing had happened.

My memories were interrupted by a startled Scrumples. The cat heard the back gate creek open and rushed out from under the table to investigate. Scrumples was more alert than any guard dog. But twice as useless.

I emerged from house to find Scrumples rubbing their face against Sebastian's open palms. Sebastian was crouched on the floor of our paved backyard. When he heard me step outside, he looked up. "Morning Hazzard," he said, grinning widely and, maybe, a little maniacally.

Chapter 15

Here he was in my home. Sebastian Grant. The last of Morgan's True Believers.

Sebastian, sender of creepy angels, and cryptic messages. Or so I thought.

He rose to his feet, scooping up Scrumples in his arms. Fickle Scrumples decided they were having none of it and wiggled free, leaping out of Sebastian's grip. Their claws left a nasty scratch across the back of his hand. "Oy, stupid cat!" he yelped.

As the grey fur flashed up the stairs, I came to their defense. "Scrumples isn't stupid, they're discerning." I switched on the warm tap at the sink. "Here, wash that cut." I opened a cupboard to find a plaster. "Scrumples knows what's up. Why are you here, Sebastian?"

He followed me inside and stuck his hand under the water. "I can't drop in on an old friend without judgment? Thanks."

"You ought to put Germolene on it too," I said, opening up a sticky-plaster so he could place it over the scratch. "Antiseptic."

"I don't need western medicine." But he still accepted the plaster. "I can pray for healing, unlike the rest of you heathens." He smiled as he said it, but I sensed he meant it.

"How's that working out for you?" I asked. "Seen a lot of miracles lately?" I knew I was repeating the same arguments Lizzie had made to me only a couple of days before. But she had been right. Besides, something about Sebastian's certainty made me more unsure than ever.

"I've seen some things." He did not elaborate. "Are you gunna put the kettle on, or what?"

A few minutes later, mug of tea in hand, we sat down to talk on the sofa in the front room. I subtly moved Oscar's files under a notebook so Sebastian could not see what they were. "Okay, let's have it," I said, turning towards him. "Why did you send me those files? Why'd you run away from Oscar's grave?"

Sebastian, who had looked confident when we sat down, faltered, confused. "What files?"

"On Christmas, with the Angel statues and the creepy snowman card in the graveyard? We saw you, tried to stop you, but you got away. I was with Lizzie."

"I don't know what you're talking about. I've not been to see Oscar for years."

"It wasn't you?" I explained about the Christmas present and the message we had found left behind on the grave.

"Harry, that wasn't me. I never sent you anything. Why would I?"

"I thought you would have agreed, we need to end it? I just assumed it was you. Who else was as invested as us?"

"Of course I wouldn't end it." Sebastian leant forward, lowering his voice. "I'm starting it."

I set down my tea. "Starting what?"

"Restarting, I should say, the worship of G, the lesser light to rule the night. Don't you see? I tried to study basic theology after Sheffield, but it never WORKED. I couldn't sum up the miracles the way we used to. I wasn't seeing healings, or transportation, or any of it. Remember how it felt? I need that again. But it doesn't work with the big God. They are too big, too distant, too far away. You can't fly that close to the sun. The Moon though. That's close. He's close." Sebastian paused, his eyes exploring mine as if searching for a clue. "He's back, you know."

No, I didn't know. I hadn't seen him. He hadn't been here in my kitchen on Christmas Eve. He wasn't a thing. That whole sect had been a scam. Even Morgan was ready to admit it. Yet here was Sebastian, trying to resurrect something the rest of us had put to death.

100

"We can do it," Sebastian said. "You and me, and the others, we will all be together at the wedding. It's going to be the best time to do it. I tried to tell Morgan, but he's too scared. I don't know if he ever believed like you and I. Have you heard his podcast?"

Sebastian placed his mug of tea on the floor so he could gesture more widely with his hands. "You and me, and Oscar, we were the true believers. The others only followed and boosted what we had, what you had actually. It's hard for me to admit, but I can't do it on my own."

I shook my head. This was the wrong direction, backward instead of forward. I was used to being overlooked now, by Rocco's family and the village who did not see me. It should have felt good to have Sebastian appeal to me directly, but the cracks had taken hold of the foundation now. I was not the one to rebuild it. "Not me. I'm not, I can't face it again." As Rocco had told me: "The past is gone, you can't live there."

Sebastian erupted to his feet, kicking his tea cup flying across the room as he twisted around so he was looming above me. I felt small, trapped against the arm and cushions of the sofa, under his gaze. "I want what you have," he growled. "I need your faith. Mine can't keep him here for long."

Sebastian pressed one of his hands flat against my chest, his other on the top of my head, pushing my face back. "I need to feel the power you felt! The power you and Dylan shared. You know what it is. You have to feel it again. You have to give it to me."

I struggled against him but he was stronger than he looked. I gasped. "Get out of here you FREAK!" I could feel something coursing through my body. Adrenaline. Fear. Definitely not power.

Sebastian snarled. "You have access to Gabriel I cannot compete with!"

He shoved me harder into the sofa by my chest. I thought he was going to crack my ribs. I felt as though the cushions were swallowing me up, surrounding me as I was pressed deeper and deeper, a black hole opening below me.

Scrumples leapt into the fray.

They jumped over me and latched onto Sebastian's thumb with their teeth as he attempted to hold me down. Never mind the tiny scratch from before, this would leave a mark.

"Stupid cat!" Sebastian yanked his hand away, gave my head one last hard shove before removing himself. He hissed at Scrumples and stormed out of the house.

Chapter 16

It took me hours to coax Scrumples out from deep under the bed where they had secluded themselves after scrambling away from Sebastian and zooming upstairs. Scrumps had the measure of the man. Clever cat. How dare Sebastian call them stupid.

"Come on out baby." I flicked a short string of tinsel under the bed and drew it out slowly, creating an alluring temptation for the cat to bat at. "Come on." Flick, drag, flick, drag. POUNCE! As soon as they were close enough I reached out and caught hold of them, scooping Scrumples into a big squeeze. "Don't you listen to that horrible man."

By the time Rocco got home in the afternoon, I had settled the cat, and myself, into a semblance of calm. He had been on a road trip with his mom Brenda to visit an elderly aunt of hers. They always made the trip between Christmas and New Year. I had not seen any of my own aunts or uncles since the big fall-out with my parents. I did not know for sure they would take my parents' side, but I assumed, and the relations had never rushed to my side, so I left them be.

I rarely dwelt on the fall out. That argument with my parents was locked far too deeply inside my memories to be worth dragging to the surface.

Rocco stomped his boots off and shook the cold out of his coat. "Its gunna snow tomorrow," he announced as he made his way into the lounge, giving the top of my head a little kiss, ruffling Scrumples' fur, and slumping into the sofa, the site of my earlier confrontation with Sebastian. I wasn't planning to mention it. How could he, a Non-Con, understand what Sebastian was trying to drag from me by force?

Rocco never understood faith as a solid, real element which exists within you. For him, the only higher power was a gentle hum vibrating throughout the universe. Ironic, considering he was the chairman of the village church fete committee.

Morgan had taught us very differently.

"We know that God made a greater light to rule the day and a lesser light to rule the night. We always talk about the Sun of God, but never the moon. What if we admit we are not worthy to face the sun directly, not without Son Glasses, not without getting burnt up! Can we approach the sun in a rocket? Absolutely not. But have we put man on the moon? Of course we have! The power of the moon is the power we can posses as men, having been made a little lower than the angels, on Earth, but within reaching distance of the angelic power, of something we can all harness by approaching the lesser light, Gabriel."

That night, I could not sleep. Scrumples was also up for hours, digging at the carpet towards the foot of the bed. He had been scratching at the same patch of floor since Christmas Eve. "Psst, what you doing?" I kept my voice low, not wanting to wake up Rocco who was deep in dreamland, sleeping on his front, a sweaty arm pressed over his pillow.

I rolled onto the floor, dropping out from under the quilt without letting too much cold air into the warm interior. I crept around the head of the bed on my hands and knees, to shoo Scrumples away from the torn carpet threads. "Will you stop that please?"

Their eyes shone back at me in the dark. On the floor, something else reflected in the dim light.

I could just pick it out, gleaming through the carpet threads. I dug my fingers around it, still partially buried, a small piece of solid material. I recognised the shape by touch, a ring. My ring. The ring which had slipped off so easily when I met Rocco and relaxed my connection to St Michaels and the past. The ring I had convinced myself was entirely made up, along with almost everything else I could remember from my time in Sheffield. Everything but the friendships was just a nightmare.

As I lifted the ring out of its embedded home, dusted off the carpet fibers and slid it back onto my finger, I recalled it all. Miracles, visions, encounters, and at the centre of it all, Gabriel.

The archangel dragged us towards him the way the moon heaves waves from the sea into tides. I had to stop Sebastian from bringing him back, no matter the cost.

Chapter 17

Snow began to fall at twelve. By morning, the side roads were covered in thick, untouched swathes of blown ice and chunks of snow. The main road out of the Tantony Edge, though gritted with salt in the night, was blocked with cars who had attempted an early dash to wherever they were heading for New Year and had instead run themselves off the road or into unmoving traffic. By mid morning, tractors were out, clearing roads, and rescuing small cars. Farmers judged the city dwellers who had attempted to dash from Manchester towards the south of England, using the road through Tantony as a shortcut.

And it had not stopped snowing. Thick flakes blew past the window as I stared out, despairing, at the carnage on the road.

Rocco was frying eggs. I could smell the toast cooking, ready to pop.

These morons should not have been on the road if they didn't know how to drive in a storm.

"All this is going to slow us down." I made my way into the kitchen as Rocco scooped the eggs with soft yolks onto buttered toast. "We need to set off soon."

Rocco laughed, but stopped when he saw how serious I was being. "We can't drive in this!" he announced. "Haven't you looked outside?"

"They can't, but we can! You are a good driver!" We have to get there. "We just have to get out of the Edge. We can go the other way. Once we are on the motorway we'll be fine!"

He shook his head. "It will stop later. People will clear out. Then we can go. Maybe. We've still got two days."

Two days till the wedding, yes, not two days to stop Sebastian. Clearly Rocco doesn't understand the urgency, doesn't know we need to settle things as soon as possible.

I started to pace up and down. "What if the snow stops, can we set off then? I can stop it." We used to change the weather all the time. Didn't we? I touch my thumb against the ring on my finger, twisting it. "Let me pray."

My concerned boyfriend hadn't touched his eggs. He was watching me worriedly. I stood in front of the window, pulling the curtains as wide open as they could go.

We used to do this. On days it was raining, when we had volunteering to do, Dylan and I would stand in the stone built porch of the church, muttering prayers. Dylan less so than me, but we would hold hands, so we could share our powers. "Keh sha le rap ah neme key sha ra!" I would repeat angelic words, letting them rip from my throat without making active choices in what to say. "Sunny skies, clear skies, sunny skies, clear skies." Often there was no change. Morgan would place a hand on our shoulders, stood behind us, dry in the doorway. "Faith the size of a mustard seed can move mountains," he would say. "You can move a cloud." I would redouble my efforts, breathing deeply and releasing everything in a steady stream of words and sounds, aiming the outpouring towards the pouring sky.

Sometimes hail would change to a drizzle, sometimes a drizzle would clear into damp air and shuffling clouds would move the rain from our area. Sometimes mist would drain away as the sun came out, burning it away. Weather changes whether we pray or not. But Morgan would insist, "Today we did it!" when the sky was clear. "He's coming though to the day! You are bringing him through."

Now, I lent forward, resting my forehead against the cold window. My words drew fog along the glass. "Kee ra shee tera skim kala ney!" I had not allowed my lungs and lips to form these sounds in a long time. It was not that I trusted Gabriel to help, but rather I knew he had to follow my words now the ring was firmly back on my finger.

My old friend Sebastian had tried to uproot the faith from within me, to capture that sense of connectedness for himself, but it was my own. I had not felt power like this since leaving Sheffield.

Rocco was concerned, his breakfast abandoned. "You don't need to," he insisted. "Give it a little time, by this afternoon we can maybe set off, don't stress."

My palms were raised, draining power from the sky. "Melting snow, heating earth, clouds are moving, snow is melting." I chanted as if overcome.

"Harry, you cannot control the weather."

"Kee ra shee tera skim kala ney!"

"Harry! HARRY!"

I felt heat burning through my hands. Liquid gold. I was moving the snow, clearing the earth. My arms were rigid and muscles tight as Rocco tried to pull them down, tried to grip onto me, to turn me away from the window towards him, to look at him.

"Harry, you can't control this. You cannot control everything about your environment! It's not healthy. It's not okay. You need to let go."

I pulled my arms away from him, to my sides, eyes flashing suddenly with anger. "It isn't about control." I was fierce, furious, then sad. "Don't you understand? It was all real, everything which happened."

Rocco shook his head. "It wasn't, no it wasn't real. It was a cult. You were caught up in a cult. You know that." He was never this resolute.

I slumped against the wall, sinking down to the floor. Rocco dropped down with me, cupping my face as I whispered, conspiratorially. "I thought the same. But I was wrong." The ring had brought it all back. The reality. "It was all real. I have got to find them. We have got to get there."

I was up, spinning away from Rocco towards the stairs as I rose to my full height. "Come with me. If we can't drive, we will get the train." I raced upstairs to find a backpack, unzipping my suitcase and moving clothing across from the holiday packing, only the few things I needed. I rolled up a jacket, shirt and trousers, the suit for the wedding, and flattened them small enough to stuff inside the bag along with some spare socks and boxers.

Rocco had followed me upstairs, slowly, cautiously. He had not been there for the Sheffield era of my life. How could I expect him to understand it now? Magic was not real here in Tantony. He had not seen it, him and his perfect extended family and fully connected neighbourhood. He had never needed it.

I pulled on boots and gloves. "Its okay, its okay. You stay here. Follow in the car when the snow clears up. I'm sorry. I have got to go. I have to go right now." It was already late in the morning. It would take a few hours to trudge through the snow to Macclesfield from here. I could take the train from there. I might still get to Edinburgh in time.

At the front door, I kissed him goodbye. He didn't want me to leave like this, but I needed to go.

"I'm sorry I scared you," I told him and meant it.

Chapter 18

The further into the storm I went, the more I knew I had made the right decision. I did not have time to wait for the weather to clear. I already spent too long waiting for storms to clear in my own mind and knew the time to make changes was now.

My thick boots crushed snow into icy mush beneath my feet as I moved along the edge of the road, following the direction of the cars. Wheels span, spitting out mud and sloppy snow water. Pale lights shone through the cloud of snowflakes which filled my vision.

Wooly bobble hat pulled down over my ears, I could hear my inner voice loudly. I was holding off the chanting words we used to repeat, "Gabriel before me, Gabriel behind, Gabriel to my left side, Gabriel to my right, Gabriel release into the day, lesser light to rule the night."

Just because I believed we had been through the most exhilarating experiences at St Michaels did not mean I trusted the source of those miracles. I was not hoping to launch G's new position as ruler of the day, but I knew I needed to link into the sense of power he had brought to me in Sheffield if I was going to keep moving, get to Edinburgh and stop Sebastian. So I battled against the chants in my head, even as I attempted to grasp onto the solid thread in my mind which linked me with the ancient guardian of the moon, or whatever he was.

By the time I reached the train station in Macclesfield, my face was frozen, my hands shivering in my gloves, but under my coat I felt hot. I had walked for hours, sweating inside a huge coat. This snow trek had not been a good idea and the storm had only gotten worse as I walked, whipping more and more wildly around me.

Shuddering through the sliding doors into the station, I pulled off my gloves with my teeth and struggled to find coins in my wallet to push through the slot into a vending machine, pressing a coffee out of it. The cup steamed. Hot liquid scalded my tongue. An employee in the ticket office judged me as I unbundled myself from my coat and stomped snow off my boots, slumping onto a bench and fiddling with my phone.

Five missed calls from Rocco. I text him. "At the station." And added, "Love you."

"All trains are delayed," the rail employee informed me as I attempted to purchase the fasted and earliest tickets to Edinburgh. He explained a train was still coming which would take me as far as Stafford on the Cross Country towards Bournemouth then I would have to take another train (West Midlands) towards Crewe. Getting off at Crewe I would have to take an Avanti West towards Edinburgh Waverley, if it wasn't cancelled. There was still no guarantee I would get there by tonight. Too many delays on the journey.

"Is there nothing going to Manchester?" Changing at Manchester Piccadilly onto the Transpennine Express would get me to Scotland with just one change.

Tomorrow, tomorrow. The employee, who seemed as though he wished he were anywhere but here, kept reminding me this was supposed to be a short storm, and to have blown over by tomorrow. He insisted normal service would resume by then.

In my experience, storms do not just blow over. They stay with you.

Maybe I could get to Manchester by coach or bus? If those weren't cancelled, I had to try, so I left the train station, dropping my coffee cup into the recycling bin on my way out. I pushed my freezing fingers back into the depths of my gloves.

A short walk took me from the trains to the bus station, a long, covered avenue filled with route maps and doors to various buses headed in different directions. I scanned the routes for something which would get me to Manchester this afternoon. A bus was leaving in five minutes. I hurried to an exit where a number of concerned looking passengers were waiting to board, unsure if the journey would be going ahead.

The driver was as frustrated as the passengers by the bus company not providing clear answers on whether it was safe to drive in the ongoing storm. "I've not been stopped by the weather yet," she told us as we stepped up on board. "Global warming is kicking all our asses."

Shivering, I scanned my card on the contactless payment machine.

Internal mechanisms screeched as the vehicle pulled away. I rested my head against the window, bones being shaken as we drove out of Macclesfield and toward the motorway where cars inched along, wipers shifting swathes of snow from their windscreens.

The heat of the bus pushed me into an uneasy sleep. My head dropped forward as I lost my footing and fell towards the surface of the moon, caught in the gravity which pulls the tides. Gabriel's gnarly fingers reached out of the dunes of dust, gripping my neck, dragging me down.

I woke up, jolting upright.

It had gone dark while I napped.

The bus driver announced we had made it to Manchester. She was done for the day. We clapped her for getting us to our destination. I got out and found myself swept by the wind into the nearest bus shelter. I knew I couldn't keep going at this rate and so I booked a hotel room near the train station.

Twisting the taps to release a stream of hot water into the hotel bath tub, I called Rocco back.

"I know what you believe is important to you," he told me. "But you can't put yourself in danger like that." He did not know the kind of danger I had already survived, and how strong I had become.

Heated like a lobster from the bath, I sank into hotel sheets and fell into a fitful sleep full of stress-fuelled nightmares.

Chapter 19

I sent Dylan a Whatsapp message from the train. "OMW." On my way.

I had woken up as a different person. I felt embarrassed about my behaviour the day before. Some days I descend and some days I ascend. This morning I had woken up with a clear head, body refreshed and ready to go to battle. Yesterday, everything inside me had felt tied to the ground, dragged down, but today I felt lifted, my chin raised in defiance. On days when my head was refreshed, the events of previous days feel small and unimportant, shrunken to manageable proportions. Maybe I had over-reacted to Sebastian asking for my help.

The roads were still not brilliant, Rocco told me when I phoned him during breakfast. He said he might not be able to set off again today. He would wait on the weather and let me know, but said I should press on to Edinburgh without him if I wanted to catch the train. Rocco told me he had called ahead yesterday to the hotel where the wedding was taking place and had changed our arrival date to today, rather than yesterday, so we had not lost the first night of our original plan.

Getting an early train would set me down in Scotland in time to warn the bride and groom of the incoming storm Sebastian.

The train creaked away from Manchester Piccadilly, slushy hail beating against the windows out of which I watched the world go by in a blur. We passed a few stations, stopping at each, before I was interrupted.

"Surprise bitch!" Dylan slid into the seat opposite me. He was drenched from his dash to catch the train from his own station once he knew which time-table I was on. After I had set off from

Manchester, he made sure to get on the same train at Preston, where he had been staying with his girlfriend over Christmas.

His grinning face felt like safety. I was anchored by his presence. "Rocco said you disappeared!" he announced. Apparently my boyfriend had text for reinforcements. "Tell me everything."

I wished I had seen him yesterday, while I could still piece everything together.

Today, the drama with Sebastian felt so much further away, like it has slipped into the side of my brain, instead of roaring at the front. "Oh you know Sebastian..." I tried to downplay it. "He always wanted to be the centre of it all." It all. "He thinks he can bring Gabriel back," I said, quietly. "Doesn't seem to realise it would be dangerous."

I did not expect Dylan to take it seriously in the way I used to and Sebastian still did, but I was honestly surprised when he laughed out loud. "Maybe it would be dangerous if Gabriel had ever been real."

His words stung.

I understood parts of our past were messy or misremembered. Lizzie had explained it clearly, but Dylan's outright denial still hit me between the ribs. Realistically, I might have said the same if someone asked me directly, yet the punch of it took my breath away. He had said it casually like it cost him nothing, while he was fishing through his backpack for a packet of Haribo. Leaving the words hanging between us, he tipped the sweets over and shook them loose, opening the packet upside down. He always said it was easier to tear open upside down. I was still stuck on what he had said before.

"You can't say he wasn't real," I insisted. "Not after everything we went through."

Dylan began to shake his head, but reconsidered, nodding instead. "Sure, a lot of what we experienced was real? I've thought about it a lot. The abuse was real. The early mornings, the hard work and I've tried to tell you for years we were getting ripped off by Morgan." Had he? "But the Gabriel stuff was bullshit."

The Gabriel, stuff? I said, "I know not everything was real, some of the miracles, but you don't remember the stuff?" I didn't know what stuff he meant exactly. But for me, the stuff meant the feeling, the moments of absolute connection we used to share between us when accessing Gabriel's power for ourselves. Not the miracles, which I knew we had maybe exaggerated the impact of in real life, but the feeling while sharing them had been ecstasy and we had both experienced it, we all had. "You and me and Sebastian, we accessed that other level because we believed, but Sebastian---." It was too late to try and recreate it now. He shouldn't try. We couldn't all be dragged back into G's world against our will.

Dylan frowned. "Harry, I…"

"The last six years have been hell." I pushed past his attempt to interrupt the flow of my thoughts. "You know as well as I do what it is like to be stuck in the in-between place, where some of it is buried, some is unclear. Finding someone else, anyone, who remembers, makes such a difference. Somebody else who experienced the level of belief."

"I didn't believe." He had set down the bag of sweets, giving our conversation his full focus. "I never believed in Morgan's bullshit about Gabriel."

What. "It was so obviously all made up."

The. "I never saw Gabriel like you did. I never spoke the angelic language."

Hell. "I'm sorry, I should have told you. I should have told you sooner."

What the hell.

I refused to accept his words. If we had not been sat opposite one another on the train, I would have backed away. The train kept moving.

"You did! You felt it, I saw you feel it. What we had, the others were jealous of, when we prayed together, it was lightning."

"That wasn't belief."

"We had a spark. When you touched me, the light of Gabriel shone so bright we BOTH burst out laughing or got thrown across the room. You're telling me you didn't feel the light in those moments?"

"Harry, I didn't feel light of Gabriel or any of that bullshit, I've been telling you. I felt love."

I was dizzy. Was this a train or a rollercoaster? I felt my stomach flip. "Love? We never dated, we never..."

Dylan was earnest as caught hold of my arms as if I were slipping away. He gripped my wrist. The tip of his thumb touched against my pulse. My fingers were caught in his sleeve. "We didn't have to," he said. "Dating was so messed up in that place. I didn't want that for us. You were too pure. I loved you so intensely and I know you loved me too because I could feel it. That was enough for me. I thought it was enough for you too."

"You loved me?" In a week of earth shattering revelations, this was apocalyptic. I remembered our first day at St Michaels, spotting him for the first time, standing out in the congregation like a spotlight had lit him up. "This whole time?"

"I love you now. I don't just love people for a while, I love them completely."

Not this. "But what about---?" His girlfriend, who he was seeing, who he spent Christmas with?

"Erin. I love her. It's different. I think we are going to move in together. I'm sorry. You look confused." He tried to explain himself. My ears were ringing. "I've got a heart too big to love one person at a time. You were always here." He slapped his palm against his chest.

I was confused. And then I was cross. "This whole time you thought Gabriel wasn't real and I was a fool for believing in him?" I skipped straight over the love thing to defend something I didn't understand.

"I never thought you were a fool, not once." He reached towards me, but I brushed his hand away. He was still speaking. "Your belief was so strong, strong enough for both of us. You took me with you, to that supreme and magic space, or whatever it was you believed. You carried me there with you."

"No. You don't get to coast on my experiences. You experienced it too!" I needed someone else to have felt what I felt, to have experienced what I went through. Otherwise…

What about the night that--?

"Harry, I only experienced OUR connection. And I loved it. Who cares about Gabriel? Not me."

I pressed my thumb against the ring on my index finger. I cared about what was real. I did not need to be told I was crazy, not by someone I cared for this much, not when the safety of our friendship group depended on my stepping up and using the powers I only had because of our connection to Gabriel. Not after everything we had lost because of him.

"Oscar." I blurted the name. I had become angry through the course of this conversation. I spat the name like blood during a boxing match. "You were there the night we lost him. You saw us lose him."

"I didn't see him." Dylan's words washed over me as he shook his head, remembering. "It was a prayer night at St Michaels, right? I remember I was happy to be there with my church family, with you. The music. The chanting. The dancing and prayers. But I

119

never followed them, not really. I was just with you guys, especially you. You always took me with you when you prayed, your faith was infectious and I was, fascinated, by you. You were perfect to me. Everything blurred out compared to you whenever we were together. It wasn't unusual for the room to disappear and the floor to drop out from under me, under all of us." His face crumpled slightly. His eyelids fluttered as he recognised the weirdness in that situation as he spoke it out loud.

He started again. His words were a rush of air, filling the space between us. "We were so tired back then. Morgan had us all in exhaustion. I think I must have fallen into a dream, with you, we were surrounded by darkness. It was the blackest night I had ever experienced, except you, you were glowing. But you always glowed when we were together. Just as suddenly we were back, back in the room, and everyone was...were they afraid? They grabbed their coats and went home. No one was speaking. They, someone, found Oscar, the next day. They found Oscar in the morning, but none of us saw him that night. He was not there."

This was too much information at once.

I had to get out of here. I had to get off the train. Where were we? I looked out the windows for an escape. We were slowing, approaching a station.

"I'm not having this..." My brain was a black hole, sucking information like a vacuum. I felt the seat behind me and the table as I pressed my palms against it. Our legs tangled as we both tried to stand up, to move out at the same time. I scooped up my backpack from the seat beside me, grabbing the shoulder strap. I needed to get off the train right away.

Dylan followed me down the aisle. I couldn't hear what he was saying, but heard the train announcer let us know where we were. "Next stop, Lancaster." I was panicking as realisation hit me.

It was me. I had dragged them all there, not Gabriel. Me.

I had to wait for the round button beside the train door to light up green before I could press it and escape. I turned back to Dylan as the doors of the train whooshed open.

"Don't follow me. I need to think."

From the platform, Dylan was a just silhouette in the doorway.

He had said he loved me. It was his love that fuelled our connection, and that connection had dragged him up with me, to the moon.

Chapter 20

A twelve-foot Christmas tree decorated with green, red and blue bulbs and ribbons loomed above me. Lancaster train station is built like a stone fortress, yet I did not feel safe.

Focusing on my environment, I was able to calm my mind a little. I knew a few facts about Lancaster. My hobby of researching individual towns and cities' queer history gave me connection wherever I found myself. I could be grounded in details.

I knew very little about Lancaster as a city, beyond its history of LGBT+ inclusion, mainly stemming from the University. I had once read about the West Road Gay Collective and how the Campaign for Homosexual Equality held their first national conference nearby in Morecombe in 1973. Activists had forced their way though crowds of angry Christians holding anti-gay slogans and signs. My own parents had never been in protest crowds, but had reacted to my coming out as if a bomb had gone off. I buried their response deeply, piling it below huge shovelfuls of devotion to St Michaels and keeping myself so busy I never allowed myself enough time to worry about the opinion of my parents. If the skeletons of those conversations ever attempted to reach me, I packed the soil down tighter and harder.

I remembered reading about a Parish Church in Lancaster where a priest had developed a service of affirmation to celebrate a person's transition, using a similar tradition to baptism and christening. It was a service designed to gently connect a person to God, and God to them. Such a link with the unknown was the opposite of the violent connection between Gabriel and me, which had thrown all my friends into danger.

We had been gathered to pray, the night of the incident, as we often did at our midweek small group, Skygazers. We used to meet in people's homes but on that occasion we had arranged to use the church centre so we had space to spread our arms and spin around. The charity work we did for the church was tiring and nights like this one rebuilt our energy and reminded us why we did everything for the church, because of how good it felt to celebrate together.

For a few months, I had been aware of an ever increasing link to the mighty being we knew as Gabriel, the lesser light, represented in the imagery of the moon, as Morgan had taught us. I had begun to feel him speaking in my mind. "You are my strength on earth. Bring me more." When I had come to St Michaels two years before, I was packing the trauma of the fight with my parents so deeply it had felt natural to press deeper into the spaces of oblivion inside me. It was from those places I brought myself into the presence of the Lesser Light.

And I had brought the others with me, that night.

Now, I found a bench where I could wait for the next Edinburgh train to pass through. Dylan might not understand why I had to get off the train, but I needed to think. The past was rushing at me so quickly, intent to repeat itself and I could not let Dylan's memory of those events distract me from my mission to stop Sebastian. I needed to know my link with the Lesser Light was real if I stood any chance to use his power again.

There was nothing I could do but wait, for now. I did not want to leave the station, and planned to catch the next train to follow Dylan on to Scotland once I had a chance to calm down. The time-table told me it would be a couple of hours before another passed through.

I made my way into the men's toilets where solid sinks, bright tiles and a wall of mirrors greeted me. I looked rough.

It had been the longest Christmas ever.

Hot water poured over my fingers as I soaped them. I could feel, more than see, the ring I had received from Gabriel gleam through the bubbles and gurgling water. I had been deep in prayer to Gabriel when the ring first appeared, filled with fear of evil and love for those with us on the mission trip who I wanted to protect.

I remembered the feeling of safety once the ring was on my finger. I was made a son of Gabriel, holding the seal of the family. I never took it off until I met Rocco. With him, I no longer needed to hold onto the protection and power (the control, Rocco would have called it) afforded by being linked to Gabriel.

Oscar was the only other person who had seen it for sure. If only he were here to verify I was not going mad. The water stopped running and I flicked my fingers to dry them.

One more glance in the mirror before leaving the –

Someone was behind me.

Sebastian.

He closed the distance between us faster than I could turn around and his fist hit the side of my face, knocking me against the stone cold sink. My head jerked back and hit the glass mirror with a sickening crack which sent spikes in every direction like a spiders' web growing out from my head through the reflective surface. In the cracked mirror, Sebastian's furious face was broken into multiples. He grabbed one of my wrists, yanking my arm upwards as he attempted to get hold of my right hand.

I was too dizzy to react other than instinctively. I clenched my hand into a fist, the ring on my index finger protected by the other digits clamping shut beside it. I pushed Sebastian back with my elbow, my shoes slipping against the tiled floor as I tried to right myself.

"Give it here!" Sebastian demanded.

He was repeating his attack from our home, but this time, Scrumples was not here to help me.

I managed to push him back far enough to gain my footing before he was on me again. I barged him with my shoulder, turning one side of my body away from him. He wrapped both arms around me, clawing at my other hand, even as I tried to keep him behind me.

"Ke ha she ra pe te kanda le sha ra ta!" Familiar sounds poured out of my mouth. I attempted to access the kind of power I used to have, back when I believed. I still believed, right? They say everyone is a believer in a crisis.

I could feel the glow of the ring extending from my finger, up and around my whole fist. A solid glove formed around my closed hand and I spun fully about, thudding my clenched fingers against Sebastian's stomach. He flew back, hitting into a toilet stall door, banging it open with his body. He growled and leapt back at me, his hands flying towards my face.

I let the substance of the protective ring shut a helmet around my head, flowing down my whole body to form armour plating.

Sebastian's attack was unrelenting, battering me across the bathroom. I kept stepping back, trying to duck his blows. He grabbed both my shoulders and swung me into one of the stalls, unbalancing me as I tripped through the door, to fall and land hard between the toilet and the bottom of the cubicle.

From the floor, I caught hold of the divider and rolled myself underneath into the next stall. Sebastian was there before me and stood on my chest, kicking my chin, knocking my head back against the bottom of the toilet.

The room span above me.

He knelt over me. "Don't be stupid, Harry," he said. "You can't stop me. I'm taking us all back there, back to him. And I need this to do it." He wrenched my arm up, prying open my fingers one by one. Whatever protection the glove had given was gone. I had lost concentration, lost connection. I was not safe.

Sebastian hauled the ring off my finger, roughly. "Now I will be the true believer." He stood up, victoriously holding his prize in the air.

Huge wings, caked with dust, lifted from either side of Sebastian's body as something rose behind him. Claws raked along his shoulders. The tall form of Gabriel lifted itself above him, a faceless head atop an enormous dragon-like body which filled the entire bathroom. Sebastian's grin was a death skull before they both disappeared.

I pulled myself to my knees and threw up into the bowl of the toilet. Everything ached. My elbows, face, neck and knees hurt. My stomach cramped from hurling and coughing into the cracked and overused porcelain toilet. The smell alone was enough to make me retch again, chucking up chunks of hotel breakfast.

I could not remember how I had ended up on the floor, puking my guts out in a train station toilet. Leaning back exhausted against a wooden stall divider covered in pen graffiti, I tried to put it together.

I had been on the train with Dylan. He told me it wasn't real. I had left the train, running, I knew that much. Something had happened since, but I was drawing a blank on the last twenty minutes. Sometimes I would find myself staring at my phone with no idea what I had been planning to look up, or great swathes of time would have passed without my realising it.

Crawling out of the stall and finding my feet, I moved to the sink to drink water directly from the tap. Not a hygienic choice, especially in a post-pandemic world. I pressed toilet paper against my lips. I brushed dirt off my jeans and picked up my bag from where it had fallen.

As I left the bathroom, the broken mirror reflected the door as it closed behind me.

Chapter 21

I arrived in Edinburgh, exhausted, but alive.

The city was a labyrinth of steps, stairs, alleyways and side streets. Black and grey buildings filled the skyline above me as I attempted to find the hotel Christine and Jeremy had chosen, walking distance from the train station, for the ceremony and the reception tomorrow, on New Years Eve.

An imposing façade opened into a bright reception lobby, filled with the warmth and glow of a thousand fairy-lights wrapped around (possibly fake) marble pillars. Comfortable chairs were loaded with red and green plush cushions. Miniature Christmas trees decorated the polished reception desks.

I spotted Jeremy across the lobby, helping his dad and brothers get checked in at reception. Following tradition, Christine and most of her family would stay at her parents home, separately, and join the rest of us here tomorrow morning as music swelled, welcoming her into the next stage of their relationship journey. Jeremy and the lads were all booked in for a meal at the hotel tonight, while Christine went out with the girls. We did not usually split our group so arbitrarily along gender lines, but some expectations stood the test of time.

"I need to talk to you." Maybe a congratulations, or an, "are you nervous to get married," would have been a better opener, but it had been quite a week. Jeremy, arms loaded with leather suitcases, studied me with a flash of guilt which smoothed into sympathy within the lines of his gentle face. I must have looked as much of a mess as I felt. He gave a half wave, half shrug, half heave of the luggage towards the onslaught of family and friends appearing around us in the hotel reception and promised we would talk, "Later?" as he hurried away.

I was disappointed not to be able to speak to him right away, but this would gave me a bit more time to sort my mind out so I could stop myself from totally unloading all over his calm personality with my erratic rants about Angels, Sebastian, the wedding and everyone at it being in sudden danger.

Being presented with the illusion of danger and unable to respond, can leave your body battered, over-filled with energy and panic response, but without the catharsis of running away or going into battle. I had once read a study, that when a rat is frightened (a science rat, under scientific conditions, apparently) it may freeze motionless in the moment, but later you can see it lay on its side, legs pumping. This action carries the energy of fear out of the body. Trapped without resolution, the unfocused energy keeps on cycling.

Getting to my own hotel room and flopping onto the bed. I felt both over-caffeinated and exhausted at the same time. I would be stuck in an energy/exhaustion loop until the mystery was solved and Sebastian stopped. Whoever had started me on this journey had a lot to answer for. I remembered Christmas morning; the angel figurine falling.

I thought about calling Dylan and trying to make up for the way I had stormed off the train, but our conversation was still too fresh. What would I even say? "I've always loved you too?" It sounded empty now. By never saying it aloud, I had kept myself protected from loss. In Rocco, I felt safe. For him, relationships are simple: You hold hands, you take care of one another, you fall asleep beside the radiator warmth of the other. Our love was a very small protective bubble in a very big world. To admit my love for Rocco, another kind of love, I would have to face the others loves I'd lost – my family, friends at St Michaels, even my once deep connection with God. I shuddered at the thought of exposing my heart like that.

Checking the time, I headed back into town to find a change of clothes before Jeremy's bachelor party tonight. In the changing rooms at H&M, I stood in front of a full length mirror in a plain white t-shirt, a blazer patterned with green triangles, and light blue jeans. I felt comfortable as myself. Dylan would have been pleased with my decision making. I did deserve something nice which made me feel seen.

Back at the hotel complex, Jeremy had rented out a private dining space with a dartboard, snooker table and jukebox. As two of his friends argued whether to play Christmas songs or Rock Ballads, (why not a Christmas Rock Ballad? The Darkness?), I tried to get a moment alone with the groom. He bubbled between friends and family, accepting their congratulations, slaps on the back, jokes and (honestly, patriarchal) comments on future married life. I didn't want to dampen the mood, so focused on the buffet of Christmas-themed snacks instead.

I piled my plate with mini Yorkshire puddings, Pigs-in-Blankets, Turkey and Cranberry sandwiches and chunky Bread and Butter pudding slices. If I was trapped here, I might as well eat. As I tucked a breadstick behind my ear and balanced a glass of Coca-Cola in one hand and plate in the other, I spotted Dylan sneak in quietly. It was unlike him to not be in the centre of the party. I wasn't sure if he felt as sheepish as I did, or was being polite by trying to give me space.

When he passed me, beside the buffet, he whispered, "Nice suit, by the way." But before I could chase him down and apologize for earlier--

"Guys, guys." Jeremy tried to silence our little group. His soft-spoken demeanour did not lend itself to announcements. He attempted to quieten the room by tapping a spoon against his bottle of Corona.

"OY!" shouted a burly man I recognised as his dad, doing the job for him.

"Thank you, Pops." Jeremy stood up on a chair so everyone could see him. "Thank you so much for coming. I know my FIANCE is making the same announcement at her bridal shower tonight. I appreciate you have all come here to celebrate two becoming one..." Jeremy made a cringe-face at the corny wording. "But we are actually going to be THREE! We are pregnant!"

A cheer erupted through the room as beer bottles were banged against table tops and the lads raced up to start the round of congratulations once again, this time with new jokes about fatherhood.

I stood alone, wondering.

Bringing a baby into the world could be enough of a motivation to want to wrap up the past. I couldn't help but wonder if it was Christine who had sent me on this path. Had she been the one to send me the angel and files at Christmas? Was it a woman at the graveyard, we had mistaken for a man? It would make sense for her to want to make peace with the past, especially with Oscar, before her wedding. I knew they had been dating not long before we lost him.

Unable to move through the crowd of friends surrounding Jeremy, and having missed the moment to speak to Dylan, I sent a text to Christine. "Where are you?"

Since most of us were equal friends with both halves of the couple we had been given a choice whether to join the Bachelor or Bacherlorette on the evening before the wedding. Gender expectations had prevailed on the most of the lads to link with Jeremy and the girls to connect with Christine, but I was comfortable enough to slip between the two.

She sent me the address of an entertainment centre and I booked a taxi to take me across town. Numerous activities were located beneath one roof including bowling, a few escape rooms, tumbling coins and claw-machines stuffed with soft toys. In the entrance, Christine bounced up to me. A pink sash announced, "Bride to Be!" and a headband decorated with plastic penises (peni?) on springs made it clear she was in the middle of a hen-do. "You made it!"

"Of course!" I air-kissed both her cheeks and congratulated her on the wedding. "And congratulations on the family!"

Christine raised her glass of orange juice in a "cheers" to herself. "Six long months till I can have bubbly, but okay…"

She led me through to the others who were waiting in line for an Axe-Throwing activity. Maybe if the boys had known the opportunity to sling wood and iron at targets was on offer at the Hen, they would have abandoned Jeremy for Christine's event.

After her turn aiming axes at a scoreboard painted with bright coloured circles around a bull's-eye, the Bride joined me at the side of the room, away from prying eyes, and I pinned her with my accusation. "I can understand why you did it," I said, abruptly. "Not wanting to carry the past into the future with your child, but you could have just asked me to look into St Michaels instead of dragging everything up!"

"Harry, what are you on about?"

"The angel ornament? The financial files? Visiting Oscar…" Now I was with her and I had seen her chucking axes, I was aware her athletic frame could easily have been the person running away and vaulting the gate at the graveyard. Everything else seemed to fit. Who else would want everything neatly tidied away before the wedding but her?

Christine shook her head. She was holding back sudden tears and I realised I had misjudged the situation completely. "I never visit Oscar! Why would you bring him up now? Tonight? Really? The night before my wedding?" I felt guilty for mentioning him now. They had been dating secretly at St Michaels, though it had not been much of a secret as we had all picked up on it quickly enough. Maybe I should not have assumed she would be thinking about him before her wedding. Maybe moments of the past do not stick with everyone the way they stick to me, repeating all the time?

"I'm sorry, I thought…"

"Harry, I'm having a good time," she hissed at me, "despite not being able to have a drink. I don't need to talk about all this right now. If I hadn't told him I didn't want to see him that night…" Her bottom lip quivered. "But I did. We had just broken up. He had become consumed by something. I said I would rather he didn't come to the meeting, cos I didn't want to see him in that state." A sob started at the bottom of her lungs and worked its way up. "I shouldn't have told him not to come, that's why he was late, why he was outside, not in with us, I…"

Lizzie was ordering a drink at the Burger Bar, beyond a few slot-machines between us and her, but must have noticed the commotion of our conversation as she abandoned her drink and zoned in on us. "Let's get you another mocktail." She glared at me, hurrying Christine away and peeking back to speak to me in a hushed tone. "Can you not? Dylan already messaged me. He said to look out for you because you were in a bad mood. Hen parties aren't about dick-straws, they are about making the Bride feel amazing and if you aren't doing that, this isn't your party right now."

I wanted to tell her about Sebastian's unhinged obsession with recreating the night we lost Oscar, but maybe she was right. This wasn't the moment. Finding myself back in the car park, I decided to walk back to the hotel, allowing both celebrations to continue without my imposition. I took out my mobile and called Dylan who did not answer and, finally, Rocco who did.

"Are you having fun?" he asked. He was planning to have an early night and set off first thing to get to the wedding on time.

"I am trying to get them to listen, but no one is paying attention to the past," I said.

"Have you considered that they are focused on the future instead?" Rocco suggested. "And maybe you should be too?"

When I got back to the hotel, most of the guests had begun to drift off to bed, and Jeremy was out front looking for me. "I'm so sorry," he said as soon as he caught me, dragging me towards one of the comfy chairs in the hotel lobby. "I didn't mean to ignore you all night. Are you okay?"

"It has been a long week," I admitted. Slumped in my seat I looked as tired as I felt, my face crumbling.

"I think I am partially responsible," Jeremy confessed. "I knew you were the only one who would be able to put all the pieces together, but I think I royally fucked up in the expectations I put on you."

Now it was my turn to be confused. Then it began to dawn on me. "It was you!"

"I sent you the angel. I hoped it would push you into asking the right questions. From what Dylan said, you have it all figured out, right?" But why? "As soon as I knew we were carrying a new life, I needed to know we had wrapped up everything from the past before we started again. I had been trying to find some evidence of what happened to us, and found the financial records online. When I saw you at the pre-party, I realised you were the person who was closest to the centre of all this back then, and you would be the one to figure it all out now. I bought the angel the next day, and dropped it at your Rocco's work on Christmas Eve, knowing it would get to you and spur you into action. I felt bad, and when I visited Oscar's grave on Boxing Day and saw you with Lizzie, I was a coward and ran away. I was worried you'd think I was a total freak, focusing on the past when we should be looking at the future."

"I get it. I get it." So it was him! Having the answers helped me to feel less lost. And I could understand it. "Being a father spurred you into protective mode."

"It was stupid. I should have just come to you."

"We've all done stupid things with the trauma we carry. There is not one rule. The way I treated Dylan, the way I literally stormed out on Rocco." I could feel other answers falling into place. "We have got what it takes to end it. But we are going to have to work together."

Chapter 22

The day the old things end and new begin.

We were all in place when Sebastian arrived, and he brought Gabriel with him.

We had decided Jeremy and Christine should go ahead with the wedding and so Dylan and I were dressed in our groomsman black suits with white shirts and yellow ties, welcoming guests to the ceremony, our eyes peeled for our old friend. We were bouncers as well as ushers, and would bounce Sebastian away on sight. Jeremy was nervous, ready to enter a new stage of his life. A couple of sips of Lagavulin Scotch Whisky had settled his nerves, but he still paced back and forth.

I had tracked Dylan down in his hotel room after speaking to Jeremy last night, and I apologised for my reaction on the train. "I over-reacted," I told him, accepting blame I didn't quite think I deserved. "You know me, it's what I do. Friends?" We had hugged it out and put a plan in motion to ensure the wedding would not be ruined. We would talk about it more another time. I still wasn't ready.

Downstairs at the hotel, on New Years Eve, a conference room had been transformed into a ceremony space, rows of chairs and a central aisle, the seats covered in white satin with green bows and red baubles, styled to represent boughs of holly. Family members were settling into place, choosing a side. There were more hats and fascinators on the bride's side than the grooms. Our friends from the Skygazers study group at St Michaels were spread evenly on both sides. We had decided not to involve anyone other than the central circle in our plan to prevent Sebastian's attempted return of Gabriel's cultish grip over our lives.

Jeremy hugged colleagues from his office who had made the trip. I was amazed so many had adjusted their New Years plans to celebrate this bride and groom. Maybe it is possible to care and be cared for by your community without a toxic dependence.

I checked my watch. It was nearly noon. Christine would arrive shortly with Lizzie as both her personal bodyguard and maid-of-honour. I exchanged a glance with Dylan. We had hoped to apprehend Sebastian before the service started but there was still no sign.

Maybe he would not show after all.

A text from Lizzie let me know they were on their way.

Five minutes.

I peeked through the conference room doors to give Jeremy a "thumbs up". He visibly relaxed. Nothing was going to go wrong.

We were located at the tail-end of a corridor and would be able to spot anyone entering. There was only one other door linked from this hall, into a small bar, currently unmanned. After the ceremony, we would all move across for arrival drinks while the ceremony room was changed into a dining area for the celebratory wedding breakfast. I had seen the hotel's waiting team buzzing about preparing the space earlier, but they had left us alone for the ceremony itself.

"Here." Another text let us know the bride had arrived. I pictured her stepping out of the car in a custom gown, her veil trailing behind her, Lizzie in a dress the same yellow as our ties, hurrying around the bonnet to lend an arm to the Bride as they entered the hotel.

A figure appeared in the corridor, sweeping towards us. Christine?

SEBASTIAN.

Tell me why he was dressed as a priest in a gold cassock, embroidered with angelic symbols up the front and down the sleeves. Talk about upstaging the bride. He seemed to think you could hide under the trappings of faith. He had his arms raised, already deeply entranced in a repetitive prayer. "Gabriel to my left side, Gabriel to my right..." He did not appear to even see us, rigidly walking toward the ceremony room, "Lesser light to rule the night..." I saw my ring on his finger, glowing.

"Here we go." Dylan closed the doors to the ceremony, as Sebastian approached. At first, he hadn't understood the threat I claimed Sebastian possessed, but he had faith in my judgment. I told him the last thing any of us needed was to be dragged back into the worship of Gabriel, and he agreed. We stood our ground.

"I don't know what he's promised you, but it's not real," I began. As he approached, I attempted to reach out and place my hand on Sebastian's outstretched arm, but he didn't slow, turning his open palm towards me and slamming me backwards into a wall as he marched on. His eyes were rolled back.

Dylan was next to attack, ducking under Sebastian's shoulder to lock his elbow around Sebastian's neck in a loop, dragging him down and backwards away from the doors of the ceremony room. I joined him, pushing myself off the wall and gripping Sebastian's left arm, helping to guide them back up the corridor as he struggled to be freed.

We stabilised him between us, moving him from the gathered friends and relatives beyond the closed doors. I hoped Lizzie and Christine would be held up at the entrance and not run into us exiting with our deluded friend.

Before we could reach the end of the hall, another figure entered. "Let him go boys!"

Morgan, out of breath and hair in disarray from running to get here on time, crashed into the corridor ahead of us. He held his phone out towards us, upside down with the microphone recording. He had a podcast on the go, transmitting live. "Listeners, I am here live with Gabriel's vessel, Sebastian, and he is carrying a message from the big man himself. Tell us, what is the vision, what message from the archangel for the fallen earth?" Morgan managed to insert himself in-between us, disrupting Dylan's grip and disentangling Sebastian who began his zombie-like walk towards the ceremony again.

I made a dive for Sebastian's feet under the cassock, attempting to trip him, but Morgan kicked at me, barely breaking the concentration of his podcaster voice. "We are coming live from Edinburgh, where the vessel of Gabriel is making his way with a visionary message for the people of God and you can be first to hear it and respond. Is he calling you to release the Lesser Light?" He was trailing Sebastian who steadily approached the wedding venue.

"Oy!" Lizzie's voice broke into the broadcast as she and Christine emerged from behind us. "Morgan, I'll give you a statement for your podcast. How about your listeners look up the company files and see how deep your corruption goes!" With Morgan momentarily distracted, Dylan and I managed to clamor to our feet and reconvene on Sebastian's strong figure, pushing him bodily through the only other door off the hallway, into the empty bar.

Sebastian stumbled against a set of wooden barstools, sending them reeling.

I slammed the door shut behind us. I knew Lizzie would finish Morgan off with a number of home truths, and with any luck, get Christine down the aisle to continue the wedding, while Dylan and I attempted to keep Sebastian occupied in here. I knew Sebastian had the advantage, though, his faith still kept him connected to the angelic Gabriel figure, while Dylan and I only had our personal strength.

140

Sebastian stopped chanting, and for a moment broke out of his reverie long enough to realise where he was. The moment he stopped chanting, Dylan drove his shoulder into Sebastian's chest, wrapping his arms around his waist to wrestle him onto the floor.

I knelt beside him, so he could hear me, as he struggled against Dylan's grip. "Whatever Gabriel has put into your head, it's not true," I insisted. "He's using you to put us all in danger!" I remembered the last time we had all been connected to Gabriel. Whatever he was, certainly not an angel, more like a trauma link drawn into the real world by our faith connection, wherever he came from, letting him wreck havoc within the our world was not the right thing to do.

For a moment, Sebastian's pupils returned to normal. He blinked free to look at us. Then he was gone, fully disappeared. Dylan stumbled as the body he was holding down vanished.

"I'm going after him!" I declared. I was sure Gabriel had taken him to the same place we had all gone years ago, to the moon. I no longer had access to G's power, but I remembered Dylan's explanation from the train. For him, it was never the power of G but the power of love, which had fuelled our connection and the electricity between us.

I turned to face him. "I am so sorry I didn't understand until now. But I think I get it. Give me your hand. I love you Dylan, and love connects."

Dylan reached out for me and the moment our skin touched, a flash of warmth and light flowed from him, up my arms, into my chest, propelling me back. Our hands released but there was a glowing string of light between us, holding the connection strong. I flickered out of existence leaving just a glowing red aurora behind.

Chapter 23

As I suspected, Sebastian was here, on the surface of the moon.

I landed, my feet firmly planted above the accumulated dust of millions of years of micrometeorites hitting the outstretched surface. Reaching into my memories, I pulled the protective armour into place. I did not have the ring this time, instead the armour flowed from the red glow of connection between Dylan, on Earth, and myself, here.

Warm light flowed up my arms as gloves merged into sleeves, over my wedding suit, wrapping fully around my body, down my legs and around my head a spacesuit helmet of light, trapping oxygen from earth and preventing my exposure to the vacuum of space. Opposite me, Sebastian stood ready for battle, in my old armour, the ring blinking rapidly where it was located on his finger. A breathing apparatus of the same material as the ring was clamped over his nose and mouth, his eyes protected by a clear facemask.

Behind him, the tall, skeletal figure of Gabriel was raised to full height, wings extended, faceless head lifted at a proud angle. The voice of the creature echoed within my head. "Welcome back."

We had been here before. The night Oscar died. When my faith in this moon based creature had raised us from Earth and dumped our whole group down on the surface of the lunar object. Back then, I had accessed enough fear and faith to extend my armour out from me and around our whole group, forming a dome over my friends.

From inside the dome of light, my friends had been paralysed with fear as Gabriel raised himself from the surface, dust streaming from his body, lifting free with a flail of his giant wingspan and floating down to touch the ground with feet that looked half-human, half-beast. Moments before, we had all been praying and chanting in St Michaels, expecting miracles and connection with Gabriel, the Lesser Light, and then suddenly we were transported here, surrounded by light reflecting off the surface, so bright it was dazzling.

For all my belief, and faith, I had never fully expected the archangel to answer my prayers and bring me here, to him. I stood before him in awe and wonder, stunned to be in his presence, shocked he had chosen me (ME!) to be brought near to him. But my faith had wavered as I began to notice where I was. The light of the sun reflected off the powdery surface like summer glinting off white sand on a beach, obscuring the pinpoint glow of stars, around us but thousands of miles away, in miniature, I could see the Earth as small as a light-up globe on a teacher's desk.

Beyond Gabriel, outside of our dome, I saw a fallen figure. Having arrived late to St Michaels, dragged up with the rest of us but not close enough to be enclosed in the safety dome of my faith armour, Oscar had fallen into the dust, all the liquid in his body bubbling away through his aghast, open mouth.

Now, I heard Gabriel speak, drawing me back into the present. "This time I will take you all." Gabriel made his announcement within my mind, speaking in a voice I recognised as my own, but deeper, different, harsher. His words were repeated in Sebastian's voice. Our three minds were connected here, mine, Gabriel's and Sebastian's.

Surrounded by the red glow of love, I strode towards them both, each step slow and steady in the thin gravity. I felt tipsy, almost weightless, outside of myself as I closed the distance between us. "Sebastian, he is lying to you. Whatever peace he has promised is false."

"It's quiet here." Sebastian's voice was a whisper in my head. Sound could not carry in space, but I heard him speaking from his armour to mine. "Everything settles here." The dust was undisturbed. "I am not bothered by my thoughts here."

I replied: "You can't hide beneath borrowed faith and never face your problems."

Behind Sebastian, Gabriel soared upwards, his wings tight against the scales of his own body as he leapt over my old frenemy, landing a few feet away from me, between my approach and Sebastian's position. His tough, scaled body looked heavy even here.

"I offered you peace, too," he said. "But you refused to receive it." I remembered Oscar's face as he lost his ability to breathe, the rest of us frozen, stunned into stillness within the dome. It was not peace he offered, it was escape.

"You never offered peace. You only stirred up fear." I felt strong. Answers continued to click into place in my mind as I realised. "You are not Gabriel, are you?" The Lesser Light was something Morgan had invented to separate us from the real world around us. "Faith in you was faith in a lie. But you, you were something tangible, something that rises from the heavy crush of trauma." An argument with my parents flashed through my head, their bitterness and clarity of position against my coming out. I had buried their comments with such force. Coal under pressure becomes a diamond. The combination of trauma, fear and faith had brought this monstrous invented creature into my reality.

Gabriel offered a peace that was not real. It was just the silence of space, not resolution, something hidden, nothing solved. For trauma to unwind it must be addressed, it must be seen, uncovered, drawn into the light of day so we can recognise it for what it is: Finished, a story come to an end, no longer controlling our choices.

As if reading my thoughts, the creature acknowledged, "I am not that puny archangel, Gabriel, you so eagerly believed in, I am Apollyon, the abyss." The faceless beast felt like an absence not a presence. "I have existed for all time, brought back every few hundred years by a person desperate to form connection but too traumatised to connect, except to me."

I had to get to Sebastian.

If I could construct armour from the love Dylan was pouring into me, surely I could form –

A sword shimmered into existence in my hand.

On Earth, in the hotel, the bar door slammed open and Rocco appeared, rushing to Dylan's side. Dylan was propped against the bar, slumped on the floor, eyes open, palms up, surrounded in a red glow. I wasn't there, nor Sebastian. Rocco dropped to his knees beside Dylan. "What's going on?"

On the moon, the creature claiming to be Apollyon reared away from my onslaught as I slashed at its featureless face. A wing attempted to wipe me out, but the dry flesh crackled as it beat against my sword, bursts of dry bone and dirt bursting from the points of connection. As I advanced, the beast backed closer to Sebastian who had not stopped chanting since the fight began. I remembered praying too, in moments of fear, repeating comforting syllables of unintelligible language.

"Don't accept his terms," I shouted. "You belong with us. Back home, safe on Earth." Now I was here, I remembered Sebastian attacking me in the train station. How had I forgotten before? Had he been persuaded by Apollyon that stealing my faith would silence his fears? I had never known Sebastian to be afraid of anything, He was always cocky and assured. But the abyss fed on unresolved trauma mixed with faith, the kind that enables cult leaders to prey on vulnerable people.

"I have never been safe," Sebastian cried out from behind the bulk of dragon between us. "It was never safe there." Whatever psychic link Apollyon held open, allowed his thoughts, my thoughts and Sebastian's thoughts to converge, showing me

Sebastian as a young child. The boy was dressed in dinosaur pyjamas, aged five or six, on his way downstairs to ask for warm milk because he could not sleep. In the kitchen, his mom was cowering beneath the weight of his dad's anger. Both parents turned to him and screamed to leave the room. His mother, voice edged with fear, his dad filled with fury.

A giant, clawed foot hit me in the head, throwing me to the ground not far from where Sebastian stood. The Apollyon stood above me, bony hands reaching toward my neck.

In the bar, Dylan was losing strength. Our connection was slipping.

I used the last of our joint strength to summon a crossbow to replace the sword and released a dart into the creature's chest. He fell away from me and I scrambled to my knees, pulling myself toward Sebastian who was aghast at the scenes, horrified by the chaos he had unleashed, but unable to move. He felt the way we all did the first time we came here. Frozen in fear. Unable to fight back. The way we had felt when Oscar was found the next day outside St Michaels, returned to the ground bruised and broken.

Young Sebastian was deep in his own past, his toes tucked into a pair of cosy Thomas the Tank Engine slippers, his ear pressed against the kitchen door as once again his parents warred. Their words were a blur, but the impact dissolved the safe edges of his childhood world. They created gaps in the safety barriers of his world now.

"It's in the past."

I chocked out the words as I stumbled closer, my hands reaching for his.

He had hidden his childhood trauma in the past for too long. It was tumbling through him into the present now. "It does not feel in the past!" Sebastian sobbed. The chemicals of negative emotion flooded his body, simulating stress reactions. He turned his hands over as if summoning something. He needed to regain control of his environment.

From behind me, the Apollyon grabbed my shoulders. He heaved me bodily off the ground and flung me into the abyss of space. I was facing the stars.

Below, Rocco's fingers were pressed to Dylan's wrist, testing his pulse. Dylan's heartbeat had begun to slow. Around him, the whole hotel appeared to shake. The light within the room changed from daytime to night as the environment outside the window switched from the city, to blank nothingness. Panes of clear glass in the window creaked, air pressure different outside to inside. Water taps screamed as the liquid inside the pipes throughout the hotel erupted without heat into gas, escaping through open faucets.

Bride and Groom and gathered family and friends felt the air begin to be sucked from the room. Christine's veil flapped frantically towards an air vent. A whirlwind was passing through, pulling the atmosphere inside out. Chandeliers shuddered. Swinging, glass crystals clinked against on another.

Pulling himself up to the windowsill, Rocco could see the hotel had been transported to the grey surface. Was this the moon? Without knowing where he was, he could see Sebastian and the creature, and further away, he saw me spinning into the abyss of space.

Dylan staggered up beside him, the brilliant glow of our connection fading. "It's you," he managed, speaking to Rocco. "He needs you to believe and love him now."

From where I was lifted, flung out towards the emptiness of space, I was twisting away, leaving the cracked hands of Apollyon. I closed my eyes. Beneath me, the hotel shuddered, barely holding together. I was barely holding together. I knew this was it, the last moments.

I reflected on Rocco, with his family and the kindness his moms had shown me at Christmas, welcoming me into their family celebrations, showering me with gifts. I thought of his dad, by the fire of crackling wrapping paper, gently probing into my life and offering insights from his own. I thought on Christine, and Jeremy, and Lizzie, and Dylan, the Skygazer community at St Michaels and the times we had spent together.

For a moment, Oscar was here too, as he was the first day the ring had appeared on my finger. He had been the only one other than me who could see it. I remembered him saying, "You will do great things." "With Gabriel?" "Or without." And he had smiled.

Something Rocco said at Christmas was clinging to me. "You don't have to be everything, all the time." But now I felt him tell me. "I want to be with you in everything, though. For all time."

Like a pulse, a new band of connection stretched from the hotel, a rope of blue light reaching towards me, joining the glow which encased my body, aligning with Dylan's love was the beat of Rocco's steadfast heart. I let my guard down and allowed myself to accept the love he offered. The glow burned brighter together.

I was tethered to the hotel on the surface of the moon.

Opening my eyes, I shared my own love with them, fully known. The bubble glow grew, expanding to surround the hotel, encasing the building in our connection and pausing the escape of atmosphere from inside.

It was time to send Apollyon back where he came from. Gripping the safety line between Rocco, Dylan and me, I willed myself back out of space, dropping rapidly.

As I crashed into the celestial body, we all reappeared on Earth, gravity kicking in, reality surging through us, drawing us back down, to the hotel, to the bar floor, the hotel returning to its foundation. It was as if we had never left.

Sebastian and I fell onto the carpet. I was up first, grabbing him by the shoulders of his cassock to heft him off the floor. He looked terrified, as if I were about to hit him, but I wrapped my arms around him, instead. I held him in a tight hug, repeating, "It is okay. It's over. You are safe. They can't get you. You're not there."

I told him, "Your parents are in the past. That story has ended. You don't have to carry that trauma. Focus on where you are now, on this moment. Can you feel me? I'm here."

Rocco and Dylan picked themselves up as well. I waved them over, and they joined me, surrounding Sebastian, their arms joining in the group hug. "You're not lost in the past, you are here."

Rocco's eyes widened as behind me, Apollyon filled the whole room. I turned toward the beast, releasing my grip on the boys as the creature's featureless face cracked in two, jagged lines appearing and separating into a ghastly hole, from which a screaming cry emerged.

"No." I commanded. "You have no power here."

The scream widened, increasing as the abyss opened deeper from inside.

I stepped towards the growing void. "I am safe. I am grounded. I am here."

I pressed my words into the expanding space. "We went though a lot, but we survived."

"I do not have to live in the past." I expressed my thoughts clearly as the emptiness ate itself, spreading outward from the increasing gap until the wings, clawed hands, beastly feet and whole body were swallowed up into its own abyss, the scream collapsing in on itself until only a pinprick of historic emptiness remained where the creature had been.

"I am here. I am now. I am loved."

150

Chapter 24

New Years Day (1 year later)

There was powdery snow on the ground, piling up against the gravestones where gusts of wind had formed mounds. It was New Years Day, a full year after the wedding, and we were gathering at Oscar's grave to pay our respects.

Lizzie arrived first, wearing an oversized cloak in dark green and hauling a wicker picnic basket which she set down beside the headstone. Crouching, she lifted out a bouquet of flowers. Red rosehips punctuated white lilies, green eucalyptus and the brown of pinecones. Winter personified. She also freed a bottle of Prosecco from the basket, and balanced six tall-stem glasses beside her on the hard ground. She buried the base of the bottle into a pile of snow as a make-shift cooler.

Following her clash with Morgan at the wedding, Lizzie had made good on her promise to report his whole organisation to the charity commission. An investigation was ongoing, but we knew it would not necessarily prevent him from rebranding. Some people will always present dangerous teaching to congregations. All we could do was make others more aware of it, and look out for one another. Speaking of people who look out for each other --

The gate to the cemetery creaked open, announcing the arrival of an upright pushchair and two proud parents. Jeremy trundled the pram down the uneven path between headstones towards the location where Lizzie stood waving. Christine leant close to his ear to whisper something and let out a bark of a laugh which echoed around graveyard. The two of them were closer than ever.

After Jeremy had shared his fear of carrying the shared trauma of the St Michaels era into their baby's life, Christine had been able to breathe a sigh of relief. She had been filled with anxious energy in the days leading up to the wedding unsure Jeremy was truly onboard with starting a family so soon. Once Jeremy had been forced to open up about the worry the past would overshadow their future, they had both been able to speak openly. Their mini-honeymoon to Oban had been accompanied with long dinners discussing, celebrating, and mourning the past.

Christine, who usually disguised her own fears with a bright and bubbly public face, had been able to openly mourn Oscar's passing and the impact it had on her at the time. Jeremy had lain pressed against her, their hands clasped, for nights of tears throughout the first few months of their married life, but after a time, she had begun to feel genuine joy in small moments again, along with genuine sadness from the past.

Jeremy parked the pram so that Christine could undo the straps to lift baby Oscar out. He looked tiny inside a puffy baby-coat, his face half hidden under a faux-fur lined hood, his mittens poking out of chunky sleeves. Christine cradled him gently in her arms before attempting to hand him over. "Say hello to Auntie Lizzie."

Auntie Lizzie was not the most baby friendly person, so was more than happy to quickly pass the bouncing baby across to--

Rocco and I, who had snuck up from the other side of the gardens. Rocco held baby Oscar while I hugged Jeremy, Christine and Lizzie. Jeremy was gleaming, "And I hear congratulations are in order for you two."

"Oh, yes!" Lizzie grabbed both our hands to look at the rings, careful not to disturb the baby Rocco was holding, hugged to his chest. We had not, subject to popular opinion, gotten engaged and absolutely did not wish to recreate last years Winter Wedding. Nonetheless, we had bought gold bands and I had changed my last name to match Rocco's family name. I had chosen to set my biological family down in the past and decided to embrace village life and not to shut everyone out. I continued to talk about queer history with people who might like it or hate it. They were entitled to their own opinions. I was just happy to share something I was passionate about with the people in my new community.

Rocco had told his moms and dad he no longer wanted to go by Richard, but would go by Rocco fulltime. He described himself as genderfull, and was on a journey of figuring out his own gender-queer identity. Unlike my parents when I came out, Rocco's moms and dad had listened and understood the ways he presented himself to the world outside of set boundaries. In a show of support, Brenda and Jennifer had even made a series of pronoun-shaped ornaments for their website's Christmas sales that year: he/him, she/her, they/them, he/they, e/eim, all 3D printed in gaudy colours, their usual brand. Maybe capitalising out of queerness was a form of celebration, for them. Rocco's dad switched to using his preferred name with the kind of ease which comes from a warm heart.

In Rocco I had found a safety rope. He understood on some days I would be unreachable, sunk into memories of my family, or extraordinary experiences at St Michaels. Sometimes I could not distinguish between what was real and what was not, but once I emerged from my funk, I was able to talk about it, and Rocco was always waiting for me, bringing me soup when I could not get out of bed. Plus I always had Scrumples curled up on the quilt beside me.

I did not have to earn my existence. I had allowed myself to relax into just existing for the time being.

As Lizzie handed around glasses, filling them with bubbles which foamed up to the brim, I asked, "Who is the sixth glass for? Dylan's in Thailand!"

Last year, Dylan had moved in with Erin and the two of them had lived together for six blissful months before breaking up. He had decided to go traveling again. He felt his gap-year was entirely missed, having devoted it to St Michaels, so this year he was going backpacking around Asia. He had a lot of love to share with the world.

"Didn't I tell you I invited--"

Sebastian.

I felt a chill run up my spine, beyond the cold. I turned around to find him stood a few meters away, as if waiting to be welcomed in. Ever since our experiences battling each other and our inner demons, it was as though we were still connected somehow. I sensed his hesitation, and stepped towards him, waving a hand to bring him closer.

Sebastian had been seeing a proper counselor and had come away from religious studies for the rest of the year, taking time to steady himself in the real world. While the others had, for the most part, forgotten exactly what occurred over Christmas (some kind of Global Warming phenomenon?), Sebastian and I had met up a few times to discuss our memories of our moments on the moon and the past horrors from our own lives which had dragged us there. The specifics were already fading, but it helped to have someone to share them with until they were past.

Trauma can reach out and take any one of us. Oscar was lost to the horrors of the abyss, and we could not go back and undo that. We gathered on New Years day to celebrate the kind of person he was. Joy-filled, warm, theatrical and kind. We all carried aspects of him with us.

Acknowledging the past as real, that bad things happen to us, and we are affected by events in our lives and the way others treat us, gave us a power we did not realise we were missing before.

It was not a power which could be branded or prayed into existence, but one we had found by living.

"To Oscar," Christine raised a glass. We all chinked our sparkling wines together and took a sip.

We would continue to live and learn and love widely.

The End